Praise for
All We Had

"Smart and unflinchingly honest and brilliantly voiced, *All We Had* is a remarkably accomplished and compelling first novel. Annie Weatherwax's other artistic persona as a visual artist has made her an instant expert at one of the most challenging but fundamental skills of a fiction writer: the ability to render the moment to moment sensual thereness of a scene. I can't wait to see what she writes next."

—Robert Olen Butler, Pulitzer Prize–winning author
of *A Good Scent from a Strange Mountain*

"The most profound insights in *All We Had* have to do with the potential hidden costs of 'economic recovery' . . . There's much to recommend this lovely debut novel, but the best of its virtues are these truths."

—Stacia L. Brown, *The Washington Post*

"Part commentary on the subprime crisis past, comic novel *All We Had* keeps you reading for its small observations."

—Leigh Newman, *O, The Oprah Magazine*

"A vivid journey into the dark side of the American Dream . . . alternates between black comedy and heartbreaking realism . . . an enjoyable read that takes an important look at economic insecurity."

—Betty J. Cotter, *Providence Journal*

"At first blush, a story about a young girl and her mother making a road trip from Los Angeles to Boston with the last few dollars they have may seem like a repeat of other novels. However, *All We Had* rises above that trend to highlight Ruthie's journey from hopelessness to hope, from being with only her mother to finding a family in a way that readers will remember long after the last page."

—*School Library Journal*

"Weatherwax's first novel is an intimate portrayal of poverty and need and a quiet commentary on American Culture. An eccentric cast of characters, from the transgender waitress to the old couple with the hardware store, add an endearing quality to this thought-provoking coming-of-age story."

—*Booklist*

"A fresh voice that sculpts with words in a way that's as beautiful as it is brutal. I love this story and the hands that crafted it."

—Patricia Cornwell

"*All We Had* is a remarkable combination of the fierce and the tender, taking the reader on the journey of a mother and daughter struggling against daunting odds to find a place they can call home. It is at its core a love story, sometimes heartbreaking, but always a strong, quiet, and powerful look at the human heart."

—Kate Alcott, *New York Times* bestselling author of *The Dressmaker* and *The Daring Ladies of Lowell*

"A remarkably authentic story of folks on the skids . . . Weatherwax's smart style, crisp narrative, sharp dialogue, and vivid descriptions send a powerful message: there is hope hidden in despair."

—*Publishers Weekly*

"Infuses gritty humor and poignancy into the story of the hardscrabble existence of a mother and daughter . . . Weatherwax's tight dialogue and short, emotionally charged scenes examine hope, the meaning of home, and the unbreakable bond of love between mother and daughter."

—Kathleen Gerard, *Shelf Awareness*

All We Had

A Novel

ANNIE WEATHERWAX

SCRIBNER

New York London Toronto Sydney New Delhi

SCRIBNER
An Imprint of Simon & Schuster, Inc.
1230 Avenue of the Americas
New York, NY 10020

Copyright © 2014 by Annie Weatherwax

First Scribner trade paperback edition August 2015

SCRIBNER and design are registered trademarks of The Gale Group, Inc.,
used under license by Simon & Schuster, Inc., the publisher of this work.

For information about special discounts for bulk purchases,
please contact Simon & Schuster Special Sales at 1-866-506-1949 or
business@simonandschuster.com.

The Simon & Schuster Speakers Bureau can bring authors to your
live event. For more information or to book an event, contact the
Simon & Schuster Speakers Bureau at 1-866-248-3049 or
visit our website at www.simonspeakers.com.

Manufactured in the United States of America

3 5 7 9 10 8 6 4 2

Library of Congress Cataloging-in-Publication Data is available.

ISBN 978-1-4767-5520-5
ISBN 978-1-4767-5522-9 (pbk)
ISBN 978-1-4767-5524-3 (ebook)

for my mother

"Where you go I will go, and where you stay I will stay. Your people will be my people and your God my God. Where you die I will die, and there I will be buried."

—Book of Ruth

Part One

Part One

CHAPTER ONE

Grit

P hil's kitchen was littered with crap. A rotisserie chicken from the convenience store down the street sat on a plate at the center of his table. It glistened and shimmered with fat as it teetered unevenly on a pile of old papers.

It was June 2005, I was thirteen. My mother had just lost one of her part-time jobs at Walgreens and another landlord was threatening to kick us out. So with her movie-star looks and Oscar-worthy acting, *voilà!* Out of nowhere, she produced Phil, an instant boyfriend with a place to live. It was my least favorite of her acts, but it always worked.

It was over 95° that day in Orange, California. The breeze from the fan in the window traveled up the chicken's spine and the remains of a few feathers quivered.

Phil sat next to my mother across from me. He reached forward, yanked off a drumstick, and the entire arrangement shook. "Mmmm, I just loooove chicken," he drawled, biting off a piece. I hated all my mother's boyfriends. Uniformly, they were jerks. This one, I decided, might also have some brain damage.

A 1-800-next-day-wall-to-wall-carpet installer, Phil claimed he could have a one-bedroom house totally carpeted in under two hours. He talked about his job as if he were a paramedic. "People need carpeting. It's important," he'd explained. "And for some, it's urgent."

Except for a trophy of thinning hair quaffed and perched on the front of his head, Phil was bald. He had a big bushy beard and his mustache grew all the way over his mouth. It squirmed on his upper lip when he chewed. It was gross.

He lived on the first floor of a run-down building on MacArthur Boulevard. His apartment smelled like carpet glue. Dark paneling was everywhere and half the ceiling was coming down.

"Oh, honey." My mother patted Phil's arm as if he were a baby. "I'm so glad you like the chicken."

You'd never know it by the way she was acting with him, but my mother was fierce and smart. She could spot an asshole from a thousand miles away and her favorite word by far was *fuck*.

"I like them earrings, too." Phil gestured, nodding and pointing his chicken leg in her direction. "They go real good with your dress."

She clutched her chest in a soap-opera swoon.

I'd seen this act a million times before. If I had to classify it, I'd call it phony melodrama. And every man my mother ever dated fell for it.

My mother finished her ogling and got up to use the bathroom. With the chicken leg in his hand, Phil stretched out his arms, yawned loudly, and showed his crooked yellow teeth.

A truck whizzed by. The house shook and a sprinkle of plaster drifted down from the ceiling like snow. Phil gazed around with a dull look and went on chewing.

I eyed him across the table.

"Psst," I whispered. He closed his mouth and looked at me.

"Yeah?" he said.

I moved closer, pulled my glasses down my nose, and looked him in the eye.

"You ever hit a woman?" I asked.

"No, ma'am." He tugged on his beard nervously. "Never hit a one."

I squinted my eyes lower. "Well, if you ever hit my mother, I'm going to set your beard on fire and watch you burn to the ground."

My mother said I was born knowing exactly what to say and do. It was a gift she didn't have.

Phil looked good and worried now. He picked his napkin up and wiped his forehead.

I withdrew. I pushed my glasses up and sat back in my seat.

"Know what happened to the last guy who hit her?" I asked.

"No, ma'am." He pulled on his beard again.

"He's dead," I stated matter-of-factly, stabbing my last piece of chicken with my fork.

One of my mother's ex-boyfriends was in fact dead, but not because I set him on fire. He died in a car crash with whiskey on his breath.

"And one other thing," I added, "the bathroom is gross. Clean up your overspray and put the seat down when you're done."

He burped. When his mustache vibrated he seemed surprised to feel it move. He wiped his mouth, put his napkin down, and looked at me.

"Fair enough," was all he said, smiling.

It sent shivers up my spine.

Clearly, Phil was an axe murderer. He probably had a freezer full of body parts hidden in a storage unit somewhere.

I searched his place for drugs and firearms. I was sure he had kiddie porn stashed inside a drawer. But I didn't find a thing. He didn't drink or yell and he went on saying nice things to my mother, about her hair, her eyes, her makeup, her clothes.

But Phil did not fool me. No matter how they started, all my mother's boyfriends turned into assholes. It was only a matter of time before he did too.

Five nights later, I was lying in bed when I heard a floorboard squeak. I listened and waited, but nothing happened. The day had never cooled; the air was dry and hot. The only window faced the street. The corner pane was boarded up.

The plumbing clattered. A speeding car outside left a *whoosh*, and a smattering of shadows spun across the walls. Then, one by one, footsteps in the hall got closer. When my door creaked open, my throat seized. A shadow loomed in the doorway and blocked out all the light.

With Alfred Hitchcock lighting and the theme from *Jaws* hammering in my head, I waited for the axe to rise. I opened my mouth to let out a bloodcurdling scream. In a perfect finale, it would echo on through the night. But then I heard a sigh.

"Push over," my mother said to me, "I can't sleep."

✧

When life was just me and her, it felt like magic. When we slept, we fit together like spoons. We'd start out with her arm wrapped around me, and in the middle of the night, like clockwork, we'd switch. It made no difference where—we could be sleeping in an alley or on a single cot, but we never crowded each other or pulled the covers off no matter how small they were.

Phil, according to her, snored. But I knew what was really going on. She missed our late-night conversations like she always did and she was bored.

That night she chitchatted like nothing was wrong. She repeated several episodes of *Roseanne* verbatim. Normally when she did this it made me crazy, but I missed her too. So I laughed at all the right parts and hung on her every word.

Finally after two nights she dropped the charade and started talking about what was really on her mind.

"Phil likes kissing too much and his penis is small." My mother never treated me like some stupid kid. We told each other everything, but this topic made me want to kill myself.

From what she'd said, the penis, I decided, was like a dim-witted dangerous child growing between the legs. But I knew when it was best to just listen. In exchange for her confidence, I remained neutral.

"I'm thinking about leaving him," she finally said one night. And even though I wanted to shout, "Halle-fucking-lujah!" I maintained my cool and nodded, expressionless. If I didn't, it could backfire. Like a stray cat, one false move and she'd be gone.

I got tired of waiting, so when Phil was on a carpet call, I took a gamble and made my move. I packed my stuff into two garbage bags and dragged them into the kitchen.

My mother was there cooking. Not in the way she usually did—by sticking already-cooked things in plastic containers into the microwave and pressing High. She was actually wearing an apron, chopping something, and trying to use the stove.

Phil had a crappy little TV with a coat-hanger antenna jammed in the corner of the kitchen counter and *Wheel of Fortune*—her favorite—was on. The image was fuzzy and blurry. It made the wheel look oblong. A plump lady in a plum dress took hold of the shape and spun it around. She bounced up and down and brought her small hands together in quick, staccato clapettes.

I cleared my throat. My mother finally turned and saw me, the knife limp in her hand.

I was tomboyish and rough around the edges, but she was classically beautiful. She had emerald eyes, flawlessly arched eyebrows, full lips, and a perfect figure. And she moved with natural grace, no matter how bad the conditions were around her.

But my mother was tired. She had me when she was sixteen, and even though she was now only twenty-nine, worry lines were beginning to define her face. In this light, her eyes were dull. The hints of gold in her light brown hair looked flat and dark. Her hair was up with her favorite tortoiseshell clip, but the clip had come loose and her hair was spilling out. She reached up and tucked a strand back in.

Her eyes slowly traveled down my arm and rested on my

bags, but she ignored me. She turned away, picked her cigarette up off the edge of the counter, took a drag, and started chopping again.

"Come on, Mom," I pleaded. "We can go somewhere nice like the beach." We were only twenty minutes from the ocean, but we'd hardly ever been. "We could get beef tacos—the crispy kind with extra cheese." I knew that's how she liked them.

There was more clapping on TV because someone bought a vowel. My mother looked to see which one.

Ding, ding, ding, ding, ding. Vanna White turned over five *e*'s.

"Come on, Mom," I said again.

My mother raised a finger (*one minute please*) as she sounded out the clue.

"*One Flew Over the Cuckoo's Nest*," I said. It was such a standard on this show.

"You know," she said, then turned and glared at me, "I really hate it when you do that. I almost had it."

"Well. I'm leaving. Are you coming or not?"

But she didn't answer. She picked up the knife—*chop, chop, chop.*

"Mom!" I stamped my foot.

"I heard you!" She slapped the knife down and turned around to look at me. "You think I like it here any more than you do? Well, I don't, but I don't have a job, and we have exactly, let me add it up"—she looked at the ceiling and pretended to calculate—"no money."

"So what?" I failed to see what else was new.

"We-have-no-money." She enunciated loudly and slowly as if I were deaf, then picked up her cigarette and sucked on the end of it so hard the hollows of her cheeks caved in.

"Fine!" I shrieked. "I'll go by myself." I grabbed my bags and dragged them toward the door.

Usually our fights escalated rapidly until we were shouting the single word *jerk* back and forth at each other, as if we were married. But this time, there was silence. The only sound was the *tick, tick, tick* of the knife on the chopping board.

"My hand is on the doorknob!" I yelled. "I'm turning it! I'm pulling the door open! Have a nice life! Good-bye, adios, arrivederci, sayonara!"

A truck sped by in front of me. An empty Bud can rattled along the curb behind it. A cloud of exhaust and the bitter smell of gasoline lingered in the street. The sun felt hot enough to burn the earth to ashes. The air was so stifling, I could barely breathe. My eyes fell out of focus. The city sounds of traffic moaned and slowed until I could hardly hear them. But the sound of my mother's knife on the cutting board grew louder. My tactics usually worked, but I feared today they wouldn't.

I took a step out the door. *Flap, flap, flap.* In the other room, the wheel of fortune spun around.

We had planned our whole lives out together. We dreamed someday we'd own a house. My version of it was always yellow with black shutters for contrast. A custom-made welcome mat would sit in front of the door with our names—Ruthie and Rita Carmichael—written in script at an angle. In my mother's version the house was white and our names were written on the mailbox. But we both agreed: our house would sit back from the road on a corner at a pleasing angle and we'd have a pool.

"Bye." I swallowed. I started to close the door behind me when her chopping stopped.

A long moment passed.

"Wait," she finally called. "I'm coming."

"Okay, that's it, come on. Let's go, move it, fast, before he gets home." I knew the drill. My mother traveled with a tattered old suitcase and two garbage bags and I was lugging her last one. She stood in the doorway and waved me on. I headed for the car but when I realized she wasn't following me, I went back and found her waddling out of the kitchen with the TV resting on her belly. "We can sell it at the pawn shop," she said.

So I looked around and grabbed the closest thing—a toilet-bowl-shaped ashtray with a figure of a man squatting over it with his pants down. "He's shitting cigarette butts," Phil had said. "Get it?"

"That's it," my mother said, "just that one thing, now let's go." I ran my ashtray out to the car and when I turned around my mother was stumbling down the walkway. She was now balancing the TV with one hand on her hip. In the other hand she carried a lamp. "I really like this." She lifted it slightly to show me. So I ran back in for another ashtray.

And, even though my mother had sworn we'd never do this again, before we knew it we were robbing him.

CHAPTER TWO

Deliverance

When I think about my mother, I think about our car—a 1993 Ford Escort. It was the only thing we owned. I was ten when we bought it from a lot on West High Street. The salesman had thick leathery skin with lines crisscrossing his face as if a kid had scribbled on him with a Sharpie.

He kept telling my mother how everything about the car was deluxe. The seats, the windows, the wipers—even the blower for the AC and heat were all high-speed and deluxe. But he had a really big lisp so the word sounded more like *de-lux-thh*. I remember the visible splatter of spit. It was gross.

My mother didn't notice, though. She was too busy admiring the car. Walking around it, coquettishly grazing her fingers over the hood.

"Do the seats go back?" she asked, batting her eyes, donning a fake Dolly Parton southern accent.

I don't know how she did it, but if just one person from Lifetime TV could see her acting, she'd become a superstar overnight.

Her performance that day was so good it took her only ten minutes.

"A woman's gotta do what a woman's gotta do," she said, emerging from his office, swaying her hips and dangling the keys off her fingertips. Back then I had no idea what that meant. "It's just the way life works," she added, which cleared up exactly nothing.

As I got older her explanations became less wordy. "I only blow them, I don't fuck them. There's a difference, you know."

We stopped and sold what we could—Phil's DVD player, sound system, and old laptop. The rest of it, the guy said, was junk. So we put it back in the car and made our way past all the neighborhood places—the laundromat where the owner shook her cane and cursed if you didn't clean the lint tray, the CASH CHECKS HERE! and CELL PHONES FOR CHEAP! place, and Glamour Glitz, where my mother once worked sweeping hair. Broken-down cars sat on cinderblocks in every other driveway. Engines, batteries, spark plugs, and cables were strewn about like guts. Brightly colored plastic baby crap cluttered the front yards of run-down houses. We rode by shacks and empty parking lots and a spattering of makeshift churches with hand-painted signs, JESUS HAS RISEN! and JESUS SAVES! and one that just had his name spray-painted at an angle across the door.

My mother loved to drive her car. There was a dent in the middle of the hood, a rattle in the trunk, and once in a while the car backfired. But she would steer it, palm open on the wheel, as if she were gliding down Hollywood Boulevard in a Cadillac.

That day, though, she looked as if she'd just buried a friend.

She sat stiff and grim in her seat. The road in front of us, littered with garbage, reflected in her sunglasses. Her jaw jutted forward. She looked straight ahead but I could tell she was seeing nothing.

"You didn't love him," I ventured.

She shook her head. "What do you think, life is one big Hallmark moment? Pfft," she sputtered. "*Love,* that's a good one."

She went back staring dismally out the window. I let some time pass before I spoke again.

"He had a pencil dick," I reminded her.

"I could have dealt with that," she said.

"His mustache was always covered with crud."

"He wiped it off," she argued.

"His crack was always showing and he had pimples on his neck."

"No, he didn't."

"Yes, he did. I saw one."

She mumbled something to herself and shook her head again.

My mother's mood could backslide fast. I waited, then tried a more subtle approach.

"You know what I think? I think our pool should have a slide."

The mere thought of having a pool could bathe my mother with light. "A pool . . ." she'd sigh, a glint twinkling in her eyes. But this time, nothing in her stirred.

"We could build an outdoor bar," I added. With this she glanced at me. "And we could get those giant umbrellas to set up everywhere."

She considered this. "Would they tilt?"

"Of course!" I said a little overenthusiastically. "We wouldn't think of having any other kind. And we could get those rafts—you know, the ones that have a place to put your cocktail."

"I love those," my mother said as I knew she would.

"It's going to be awesome. We'll put a cabana on one end and a snack bar on the other and maybe we'll have a diving board, too."

A few minutes went by. We were driving under the overpass to Route 57. The beams above were streaked with bird shit, some of it dripping and wet.

"You know what . . ." she said. She pulled the car over, put it in park, took her sunglasses off, and twisted in her seat to look at me. Through the seam in the pavement above us a sliver of light fell across her face. It flickered like a strobe as the cars *thump-thump-thumped* overhead.

"I've been thinking. You're right. I think it's time for a change of scenery. What are we waiting for? We have a car and we have money now." It was true, we got $950 for Phil's stuff and we hardly ever had that kind of ready cash. "And you know what else?" my mother added. "I think it's time you and I head to Boston. We're going to end up there anyway."

My mother was not certain about much, but one thing she knew for sure was that I was smart enough to get into any college, and Boston, according to her, had all the best schools.

She and I had lived on and off the street, or in shelters. We moved in and out with boyfriends—sometimes with breathtaking speed. The few times that we could afford to rent our own apartment never lasted. Even when my mother worked four jobs, it was hard for us to pay our rent. And we never stayed in one place for more than six months. But I hardly ever missed a day of school. She made certain that every school system knew who I was and where the bus should pick me up.

"Yup." My mother nodded, agreeing with herself. "Harvard is going to hand you a scholarship, I just know they are."

I didn't really see how I'd end up in college, but the thought of it could bring her out of any slump.

"Maybe when I graduate, I'll become a doctor," I said.

"Oh my God. I was just thinking the same thing. You'd make an excellent one."

A smattering of garbage blew down the street and sprinkled the hood of the car. She grabbed her pack of cigarettes off the dashboard, lit one, then pitched the match out the window. "I'm even thinking that when we get to Boston," she said, shifting the car into gear, "once and for all"—she took a long hard drag—"I'm going to quit smoking." She blew the smoke sideways out the window. "Dammit, let's do it." She stepped on the gas and we drove out from under the dark overpass and into the light of the wide-open freeway.

We went from zero to sixty in no time. I was out of school and she was out of work. We had no place to be and not a thing to lose.

With the windows open, strands of my mother's hair flicked and flashed in the sunlight, trailing behind her like ribbons. In between places was my favorite place to be. With the past behind us and the promise of better things ahead, few things ever felt as good.

I stuck my head out the window. The rush of air whipped around my face, flapped my lips, and made my eyelids flutter.

Gas tanks and power grids raced by. Mounds of gravel zig-zagged across the earth and cranes punctuated the sky at sharp angles. When the city receded in my mirror, it couldn't go fast enough.

My mother glanced over at me and smiled. She reached forward, pushed a CD into the player, and turned the volume up.

"*We—are—fam-i-ly. I got all my sisters with me!*" Sister Sledge—our favorite and the theme song to our lives—blared out. We swayed and sang the lyrics at the top of our lungs. The freeway widened, the landscape emptied out. The engine hummed and I pictured the car lifting off the ground. We'd sail across mountains and by clouds, we'd dip in and out with the birds. "Look, there's China!" I'd shout. We'd hover just long enough to wave at all the people. Then we'd surge into orbit, leaving only the rush of sound and a white, wavy streak in the sky behind us.

This was how our story always went. With the wind at our backs we soared like bandits narrowly escaping through the night. And no matter where life took us or how hard and fast the ride, we landed and we always stayed together.

Daylight faded. The sky became a show of waning color. Yellows shimmered into blues. The sun singed the underside of clouds with orange. Poetry was everywhere.

Then, *boom!*—the car backfired. A burst of sparks erupted from the tailpipe.

"Oh my God!" I yelled. "We're on fire!" My mother looked in her rearview mirror. When she swerved off the road and slammed on the brakes, an assortment of Phil's shit went flying.

She grabbed her purse and we both jumped out. Smoke poured from the back end. My mother thought fast. She clicked in her heels to the passenger side of the car, ducked in the window, and grabbed her supersize Diet Coke from the holder.

"Stand back!" she yelled. In a single dramatic motion, she chucked the top on the ground and pitched the Coke at the muffler.

With a startling pop and a hiss, a giant vaporous cloud enveloped us and we doubled over choking. My mother took her bag off her shoulder, covered her mouth, and coughed into it.

Her purse was black vinyl, and oddly shaped like a giant pork chop. She never went anywhere without it and, like a man with a Swiss army knife, she used it for everything. She jammed parking meters and fixed vending machines by batting them hard on the side with her bag. I'd seen her use it as a weapon. She'd wind it up, let it go, and with the shoulder straps flying, it'd spin through the air until *bam!* she'd hit her target every time. She used it as a pillow on the bus. She swatted flies and shaded her eyes from the sun with it. I'd seen her hold it up against the wind and rest it on her head when it rained. And sometimes it just punctuated her mood. She'd fling it fast and hard on the ground, or lob it, tired and slow, on the couch.

"For Chrissake." She flapped her bag up and down this time, using it as a fan.

"Really," I coughed, "who knew Diet Coke was so toxic?"

Once it was safe, my mother inched her way forward. Clutching her purse, she bent over slowly and peered underneath the car.

It was almost dark by then. The freeway had quieted. A warble of insects pulsed through the air.

"The muffler's dragging on the ground," my mother reported from her bent-over position. She stood up and pushed her bag back on her shoulder. She put the key in the trunk. It popped and with a creak, slowly opened.

When we robbed Phil, we ended up with a lot of worthless stuff like his coffee mugs that said MY LOVE IS LIKE DIARRHEA, I CAN'T HOLD IT IN. "Collector's items," he'd claimed. We stole his blender that only worked when the kitchen light was on and his toaster that set the toast on fire if you didn't dig it out.

But the only thing we took that I really wanted weighed a thousand pounds. In the patch of dirt and dead grass in front of Phil's building I'd found a cement statue of the Virgin Mary. She was lying on her back with bird shit on her forehead.

When I grow up, I want to be a preacher so I can set the record straight. Religion is a hoax and when I read the Bible, I really *did not* like it. The characters were all flat, the dialogue was bad, and the imbalance of power cheapened the plot. In my version, Mary would play a bigger role. She'd rise up, take control, and set the world straight. As it is, she's just written right out of the book, which for me was like killing off the movie star in the very first act. I wrote a paper on this topic for class and got an A-plus-plus on it.

I collected Mother Mary figurines. I had a string of plastic Mary lights that blinked on and off when you plugged them in. I found a porcelain one on the street in perfect condition, and I had a teeny-tiny hand-blown glass piece that I kept in a cardboard jewelry box. My favorite, though, was the Mary I had glued to our dashboard. Her eyes rolled back into her head as if she found life endlessly boring. There were others, but none as big as the one lying in our trunk.

The streetlight cast her cement-gray complexion a cold and stony blue. A swirl of lingering smoke drifted by her. A dog

barked in the distance. A breeze kicked up on the freeway behind us and sprinkled Mary with dust. I picked up a rock and
threw it just to watch it sail through the air and hear it drop.

"I'm sorry, Ruthie." My mother laid a hand on my shoulder.
"But the weight of her is dragging us down."

We left the Holy Mother facing the road. Backlit by a line of
trees, her outline glowed. She gazed upward toward heaven—
waiting, it seemed, for a ray of light to deliver her from evil and
take her home.

CHAPTER THREE

Flesh

Hours passed and we kept going. We made it to Utah that first day. It was almost midnight when my mother got off the highway and pulled over on an empty country road. She turned the key, the headlights went out and a slick of flat black inked out all the stars. Not a single pinprick of light showed through.

Halfway in a ditch, we'd spent the night at an angle and in the morning I was crammed up against my door. I sat up and looked around disoriented. An ancient billboard loomed in front of us, scraps of old ads peeling up in scales of faded color. Four rusted posts sat in hooves of crumbling cement like something prehistoric.

My mother was still sleeping when a dark cloud above us tore open and the rain fell. It surged and swelled and streaked across the sky in angled sheets of gray. But as quickly as it fell, it evaporated. Then it stopped. The road sizzled in its wake and a hush of steamy fog roamed across the earth. A flock of birds landed in the field next to us and started pecking for worms.

My mother finally woke. She stretched and yawned in her seat. When she was done, she tapped me on the thigh, as if to say she was glad to see me. With her foot, she pushed open her car door and got out.

She stood on the side of the road, looked out at the field, and stretched a bit more. She was wearing her usual outfit—tight jeans, high heels, and a tube top.

The first rays of sun pierced the clouds, she lifted her face and parted her lips as if trying to drink the light. She reached inside her pocket for a hair tie, twisted her hair into a bun, then hoisted up her tube top. When she stepped off the road, the birds rose up. Dipping their wings in unison, they banked in the air and in one synchronized motion, they landed on the edge of the billboard. Lifting their little rumps, they settled down, then looked around like they were bored.

My mother walked a few feet into the field. She unbuttoned her jeans, pulled them down, and squatted on the ground.

She and I almost never had privacy—from each other or anyone around us. The nicest place we ever lived had a shared bathroom without a door. She'd stopped caring about stuff like that. "Even the queen shits," she'd said to me once when she was squatting in a bush.

My mother didn't know it, but she deserved a nice bathroom. If I could give one to her, it would be grand and made of marble, suitable for Cleopatra. Pillars would rise at the corners of a sunken tub. I would travel to the Dead Sea, by camel if I had to, just to bring her back an urn of healing salts—if only for twenty minutes, she could float weightless in a bath of warm water, relieved of all her pains.

A sliver of light cut across my mother's back. She reached between her legs and pulled her tampon out. She flung it by the tail as if it were a rat and replaced it with a new one.

"Hey," my mother said when she made it back to the car. "You ready?"

She settled in her seat, stuck the key into the ignition, looked at me, then stopped.

"Are you okay?" she asked.

A lump rose in my throat. My eyes welled. "I'm just hot." If there was one thing my mother never wanted, it was pity.

"Here." She reached over the seat, felt around, then pulled up a half-filled bottle of water and handed it to me. "Have some."

She went to go turn the key again.

"Mom?"

"Yeah." She looked at me.

I searched her face. The lines between her eyebrows were deeper than I remembered. Her lips were creased and chapped. Her red fingernail polish was almost all chipped off.

"Nothing." I swallowed hard.

She glanced at me and sighed. She smiled just a bit. Then she reached across the seat and stroked my forehead.

"You'll cool off," she said.

The wheels spun. The car rocked back and forth, and with a grinding grunt, we drove out from the ditch and into the sun.

The heat pummeled down in blistering rays. The earth looked left for dead. The "deluxe" air-conditioning in our car never worked. Even at sixty miles per hour, the wind through our open windows couldn't cool us off. The highway threaded through a quilt of bone-dry barren fields. Wavelengths of telephone wires were punctuated with sickly looking birds.

We drove clear across Utah and through the mountains of Colorado. We slept on the side of the road or in rest areas. Twice the cops woke us up and told us to move on. We took sponge baths in gas-station bathrooms, we ate at McDonald's, and when we got sick of that we ate snack food: chips and Cheez-Its, Doritos and nuts. And always we drank Diet Cokes.

Halfway through Nebraska on I-80, my mother's toothache flared up. She'd had one on and off for months. When it hurt, it hurt so bad she had to wear sunglasses even in the dark. The toothache had always gone away, but this time was different. Her mouth was bleeding and the pain went all across her face.

She stuffed napkins and toilet paper inside her cheek. She stopped the car and lay across the seat with her head upside down out the door. We bought her bourbon and Advil—a combination, according to her, that could cure almost anything. But nothing could stop the bleeding, and the pain was only getting worse.

My mother found a gas station, parked the car, and pulled me into the dingy bathroom. She held the edge of the sink, squeezed her eyes shut, thrust her wide-open mouth at me, and waited there. I had no idea what she was doing until she opened one eye, then both, and said, "Don't just stand there. God help me and pull it out."

Except to say things like "God, this sucks!" or "God, I hate this," the only time my mother ever mentioned God was to say that he'd given her good teeth. Now it seemed she was losing even that.

"Ruthie," she pleaded when I didn't move. She grabbed my hands and held them. "Please. I can't do this myself."

Her face was swollen. Her cheek throbbed in and out. Her eyes were bloodshot, her skin blotchy and red. There was a scab above her brow, from what, I couldn't remember.

She dropped my hands, opened her mouth, and squeezed her eyes shut again. And I realized I had no choice. I had to pull her tooth out and I had to do it fast.

I held my breath and looked inside her mouth. It was wet and red and her tongue was swollen. It smelled like cigarettes and bourbon and blood. My knees shook. My vision blurred. Her mouth zoomed in and out of focus, the scale of it shifted. It felt as if I might lose my balance and tumble deep down inside my mother's throat.

I steadied myself on the edge of the sink, closed my eyes, and swallowed. A bead of sweat rolled down my forehead and settled in the corner of my eye. I pushed my sleeve up and like a farmer reaching inside a cow, I stuck my hand into my mother's mouth. The tooth was in the back. It was loose and slick with blood. The stench of someone else's bowel movement lingered in the stifling air.

"I'm sorry, Mom." There were so many things to be sorry for. But this was how we lived—with pain and foul smells.

I clenched my jaw, held my breath, and dug my fingers underneath her gum. The tearing of her flesh was audible. My mother moaned. But I knew I couldn't stop. I braced a hand on her shoulder and yanked. The tooth flew out behind me. She stumbled backwards, hit the wall, slid down, and landed with her legs spread-eagle on the floor. Her eyes rolled back, her head fell forward. She took one long gasp of air. A line of bloody saliva ran down the corner of her mouth. The back of her head started bleeding where she'd hit the wall.

"Mom!" I fell to my knees in front of her and shook her, but there was no response.

I took her head and with my bare hand, applied pressure where it was bleeding.

"Wake up, Mom. Please." I cradled my mother and rocked her.

I did not believe in him, but God, they say, is everywhere. I looked around this nasty bathroom. "Please," I prayed to him. I lived in fear of losing her. Every time she closed her eyes to sleep, I worried she'd stop breathing.

I was tough. I almost never cried, but when my mother groaned I started weeping.

"It's okay," she said. She reached a hand up and held my cheek. "I'm here."

I folded up some paper towel into a tight square and had her bite down hard on it. When the cut on the back of her head stopped bleeding, I helped her up and washed her hair.

She splashed her face with water and I rinsed mine, too. We braced ourselves on the edge of the sink.

"Come here," she used to say when I was a kid. Pressing our cheeks together in front of a mirror, she'd first pucker up and examine her pout from all angles. Then she'd hold my face and study my lips.

"Yup, you got my mouth. And let me see those eyes." I'd raise my eyebrows in an effort not to blink. "Yup," she'd say, and drop my face. "When you get older we are going to look just like sisters."

But I could never see it. She and I were opposites. I had short, coarse hair; hers was long and silky. Her figure was curvaceous and feminine, mine was lean and hard. I wore jeans with high-tops and she wore hers with heels. But in the dismal light of that bathroom, as we looked at each other in the mirror, I saw a sadness in our eyes and a weariness around our lips that we shared.

We heard pounding at the door.

"What the hell is going on in there?" a woman yelled.

"Just a minute." I tried to sound normal. I hurriedly wiped the blood off the floor.

"I'm going to call the police if you don't open up," the voice outside shouted.

When we opened the door, a squat woman in a pleated skirt and wide-brimmed hat stood in front of us, fist raised mid-knock. With purse in hand, she clutched a small boy in front of her. He was wearing a Cub Scout uniform—kneesocks, suspenders, shorts, and a beanie.

"There's a line out here, you know!" the lady scolded, even though there wasn't.

I held my mother upright and guided her out the door.

"Trash," the woman muttered as she steered the boy past us.

"Bitch," I muttered back.

CHAPTER FOUR

Anger

O n the outskirts of Chicago the miles of pitch-black high-way divided and strip malls appeared on both sides. Neon signs streaked by like finger paints smeared on walls. A dazzle of reflections flew off the hood of the car. And as quickly as the carnival of color erupted, it faded and the world outside my window was cast again in shades of black and gray.

We crossed over Indiana through miles of brittle desolate earth. Every day when the sun went down it melted into a blazing pool of orange. It shimmered on the horizon and when it finally slipped away, a scar of bluish purple bruised the earth for hours. And the heat lingered on.

We spent a night behind a supermarket and in the morning, a box of strawberry Pop-Tarts was just sitting on the ground in front of us as if a fairy had left them there. The sun had even warmed them up.

By the time we reached Pennsylvania we'd been on the road for almost seven days. And all the things my mother usually did—tapping the steering wheel with her thumbs when she liked a song, biting her bottom lip when she wasn't smoking—suddenly annoyed me. We tried playing Sister Sledge again, but the original effect of "We Are Family" had reversed itself. Now the last thing we wanted to be was related. On top of that, something in the car smelled. We sniffed around but never found the source. We rolled the windows up and down—it was unpredictable, which made it worse. It could stink like blue cheese or baby vomit. When we finally entered New York State it smelled like both.

By ten P.M. we were hungry and tired and hot. We'd finished the last of our Pop-Tarts hours before. We needed air-conditioning and food.

A truck whizzed by towing a blinking traffic arrow. For twenty miles it was all we saw. The deserted highway went on and on forever. The posts on the guardrail *whooshed* as we passed them. A stone caught in our tire *tick-tick-ticked* against the pavement. I felt as if we were standing still and the landscape out my window was merely scrolling by.

"Look!" my mother said, pointing out the window. A glowing sign emerged from the darkness like a pool of water in the desert. GAS, FOOD, LODGING, it read, so we took the exit.

A heavyset, bucktoothed, chinless girl sat in the toll booth at the bottom of the ramp.

"Two fifty," she said, too busy reading *People* magazine to look at us. With her weight on one hip, she stuck her hand out and chomped on her gum. Her plump fingers wiggled impatiently as my mother dug inside her purse.

With a huff, the girl put her magazine down and rolled her eyes when my mother handed her a fistful of change.

"Pfft," I said as we pulled away. "What was her problem?"

My mother wasn't listening. She was still pawing through her bag. "What happened to all our money?" she asked. "Here, you look." And she thrust the bag at me. "There's got to be at least another hundred in there somewhere."

My mother's bag was more like a sac. It had no zippered compartments and looking into it was like looking into a black hole. The only way to find anything was to feel around at the bottom. So I yanked it open and shoved my hand in.

Neither one of us had kept track of our money, and my mother didn't use a wallet. She just took fistfuls of whatever change was handed to her and stuffed it in her purse.

Life took a nose dive when I couldn't feel a single coin.

"Dump it out," she commanded.

"Seriously?"

"You heard me," she said. "Just do it." There was so much crap inside her bag it was scary. But she was in a frenzy. So I turned it over and a whole store of things spilled out.

lipstick
rouge
matches
cotton balls
fingernail polish and remover
fingernail clippers
cuticle trimmer
a toothbrush
a hairbrush
an eyebrow brush
a pad of paper
twelve paper clips

All We Had

eight bobby pins
three hair clips
eight hair ties
an extension cord with a curling iron attached to it
several crushed cigarettes
three packs of matches
five Bic lighters
a blow dryer
two tubes of mascara
eyeliner
eyelash curler
three compacts
two packs of cigarettes
six plastic straws, two paper ones
two ketchup and three mustard packets
three plastic spoons and a stainless-steel fork
bottle caps
a street map of Orange, California
a crumpled-up Dunkin' Donuts napkin
numerous tampons both in and out of their wrappers
a tea bag
shoelaces
tweezers
a bottle opener
a can opener
a wine opener
a pair of scissors
travel-size shampoo and hand cream
Noxzema
a razor

Krazy Glue
wire cutters
a screwdriver
three pens, one magic marker, and six pencils

One by one, I cataloged each item and replaced them in her bag. My mother took quick sharp looks in my direction. "Keep going," she snapped. "I know there's money in there somewhere."

She'd been keeping an open bottle of bourbon between her legs ever since I pulled her tooth out. She'd sip it every time she felt pain. But now she swigged it with abandon. Her face glowed dim in the light of the dashboard. Beads of sweat glistened on her upper lip. She gripped the wheel, her knuckles turned white.

She was going to snap, and it was not going to be pretty. I unbuckled my seat belt, maneuvered to the back, and started scouring the seat and floor. I looked everywhere, and when I finished we had a twenty-dollar bill, two fives, four singles, and three dollars and thirty-eight cents in change.

"That can't be it," my mother muttered. She swerved off the road and screeched to a stop. She got out, stomped around, and flung my door open.

"Move it!" She pulled my arm.

I jumped out and stood back. When she was like this I'd have to steel myself to get through it.

She pawed through the garbage on the floor. Paper cups, napkins, wrappers, empty Coke cans flew out behind her like dirt. When she started on the backseat, a barrage of Phil's crap sprayed the ground like bullets. One by one the diarrhea mugs went flying. "Piece of shit anyway," my mother mumbled, whipping an ashtray to the ground behind her.

By the end, the only thing that survived was Phil's TV. She'd tried but couldn't get it out. Wedged between the back of her seat and the floor, she left it looking as if it needed an ambulance. The antenna was mangled, the screen all scratched up.

My mother stood up. She was wild-eyed and panting, her hair a furious mess. She tossed her hands up and shook them. "Fuuuuuuuuck!" she howled.

Then she stomped back to the driver's-side door, yanked it open, got in, and slammed it.

I stood next to the car, waiting, hoping she'd cool off a bit. There were no streetlights, but the moon glowed so bright it was almost garish.

"Get in!" she screamed.

I slid into my seat, squeezed the armrest on the door, and braced myself. And then it really started.

"You know," she snarled. She twisted the rearview mirror so she could see herself, then tore her bag open on her lap and began rummaging through it. She pulled out her brush. She whipped her head—*back and forth, back and forth*—and yanked her brush through her hair. "I don't know why I ever listen to you." She pitched the brush back into her bag and fished out a compact. She popped it open, picked up the powder puff, and in a fury spanked it all over her face. She snapped the compact closed with one hand and exchanged it for another one. This time she stabbed a brush into the makeup, and with the same swinging head motion she turned her cheeks and swirled rouge on each one.

"We should have just stayed with Phil!" She'd unearthed her mascara and was pumping the little wand in and out frantically. "I mean, he had a *job* and a *yard* and a *home!*" She screamed all the nouns, simultaneously jerking her head and shoving a wide-open eyeball up to the mirror, applying black to her lashes.

"I tell you, that is the last time I ever let you talk me into doing anything! Do you hear me? Do you?"

My face got hot; my ears were burning.

"You're all I've got to bank on," she used to say to me. I hardly ever failed her, so when she talked to me like this, it hurt. I pinched my arm hard to keep from feeling anything.

She jammed the wand back inside its tube and pulled out her lipstick. In a sharp nasal tone, with her lips in an O, she mumbled a few more swears. She finally threw the last of her makeup back into the bag and flung it behind her where it hit the rear window with a *thud*. As she grabbed her cigarettes off the dashboard, her hands trembled. She broke the first two before she got one out. The third one quaked between her lips as she fumbled with her lighter. *Flick, flick, flick.* When she finally lit it, she took one long drag and half the cigarette burned down. She tilted her head and through pinched angry lips she exhaled a line of smoke that bounced off the ceiling and engulfed her.

"You know what else?" she said smugly. "I'm sick of looking at that stupid nun on the dashboard." She pointed at Mary. "It's Catholic-white-trashy and you should've outgrown it by now."

Snap, snap, snap. There was hardly anything left of them, but I gnawed at my fingernails anyway. She'd crossed a line and she knew it. I never believed in fairy tales or Santa Claus. I did not believe in God or Jesus. I believed in Mary.

I rummaged through the glove compartment and found some

gum. I crammed two pieces in my mouth and started chewing. But less than thirty seconds into it, I remembered: I hated gum. It was tiresome and tedious and the flavor never lasted. So I spit it out. I went through the whole pack that way, then crumpled up the empty wrapper and threw it on the floor.

My mother had blown off all her steam and was now acting as if nothing had happened. Her arm was draped casually out the window. Another cigarette dangled between her fingers. She eased up on the gas and her shoulders dropped. She swiped a wisp of hair from her forehead and tucked it behind her ear.

"Phew," she said. Extending her arm, she let the wind snatch her cigarette butt. "Thank God." She turned her palm faceup. "Finally . . . a breeze."

My mother prattled on for at least a half hour about how dry and hot the summer was but I didn't listen. I stared out the window. The broken divider line stitched down the center of the road and the headlights pierced the darkness at always the same distance in front of us. In the heat the insects seemed to multiply, complaining loudly as they hit our windshield. My mother flicked the wipers on and smacked away their juice.

Then finally at a red light, the street ended.

"Hmm, let's see," my mother mused, inching slowly forward. I looked at Mary and her eyes rolled back into her head, perfectly capturing my mood.

"If you were a 7-Eleven, which way would you be? Would you be right?" She sat up and looked past me out the window. "Or would you be left?" She turned and looked in the opposite direction.

WELCOME TO FAT RIVER! a sign exclaimed. Across from us the street was peppered with half-vacant storefronts.

"What do you think?" my mother asked.

The red light squeaked and swung on the wire overhead. An inflated Walmart bag skipped along the road on its handles, but not a single car went by.

"Huh?" she asked again, and for the first time since her fit, she glanced at me. "Hey." She patted me on the leg as if she hadn't just been mad at me. "Don't be so glum. We'll be okay."

The light turned green and my mother looked forward.

"I promise," she added.

With her palm open on the steering wheel, she glided the car right, rounding the corner smoothly, as if she'd known all along exactly which way to go.

A few miles down the road we found a gas station with a diner next to it, and they both looked open.

"I told you things would get better, didn't I?" my mother said, as if she'd put this scene in place herself.

Tiny's Grub 'n' Go! had a spinning neon sign out front. The letters flashed one at a time, spelling out the name. The *o* quivered and made the exclamation point look twice as bright.

My mother turned the wheel and the gravel in the parking lot crunched. "I'm starving," she groaned.

She threw her car keys in her bag, shoved her purse on her shoulder, and got out. She was almost running through the parking lot.

"Let's just hope this place is really open," she said as I followed her. "Cross your fingers." She raised her hand to show me hers already were.

A neon chicken wing flapped up and down in the front window and a hot dog flashed in and out of its bun. Blinking colored lights outlined the plate-glass windows. The warm hum of electricity stroked the air.

My mother took the few steps up.

"Yes!" she breathed when the breezeway door flew open. At the door to the restaurant she took a deep breath and gave it a yank.

"*Fuuuck!*" My mother hawked the word out from the back of her throat. It was locked.

She cupped her hands around her eyes and peeked in. I did the same next to her. A plastic jack-o'-lantern sat by the register, a string of tiny American flags hung above the counter, and a fake Christmas tree stood just inside the door as if here all the holidays happened at once.

Karen Carpenter crooned from the stereo. "*Why do birds suddenly appear . . .*" In the dim light we saw a waitress wiping down the counter. In big, rhythmic strokes she performed the song with her rag.

My mother slapped her palm on the door and rattled the handle, but the waitress didn't hear us, so my mother pounded harder. The waitress finally looked up and turned the music down.

"Please," my mother said through the door, exaggerating her mouth and holding her hands in prayer. "I have a kid," she added pointing to me.

My mother and I were more like best friends. The word *kid* just didn't fit for me. But I knew this routine. I smoothed out my T-shirt, and with my best innocent look I stood on my tip-toes and made sure the waitress could see me.

A man peered out the service window as the waitress pointed us out to him. He nodded his head, and, fishing her keys out of her apron, the waitress headed for the door.

"Oh, thank Christ," my mother said when the door opened. "We've been driving for *hours*."

"Don't sweat it, honey," the waitress said, holding the door open for us. "Just follow me."

Up close the waitress was taller than she'd first seemed. Her large hands swung back and forth by her side like a monkey's. Her shoulders were broad and her voice was deep. Her hair was uniformly blonde, stiff, and shoulder length with a perfect flip curl. She swayed her hips exaggeratedly, the way you would when you were only pretending to have them. And her feet were huge. You should have seen her red mules—they were like boats.

We slid into a booth by the window and I looked up at her. Her eyes were framed by enormous fake lashes that curled up at the corners like a cat's. And she also had a mustache—not the kind you'd bleach to hide. Hers was a deliberate and grand handlebar with the tips waxed up into an elaborate set of curls.

"We normally close at eleven." She slid a couple of menus across the table. "But lucky for you the boss is a real mensch."

"Oh my God, are you Jewish?" I asked excitedly, recognizing the Yiddish. I *loved* the Jewish people. They were the only sympathetic characters in the Bible and Yiddish was my favorite language. *Farkakt* and *farklemt*, I mean, who couldn't love those words? Just saying them was fun. "*Farkakt!*" "*Farklemt!*" "*Farkakt!*" "*Farklemt!*" If I could, I'd make Marco Polo a Yiddish game.

The waitress gasped. She drew her big hand delicately to her chest and stooped in toward us. "Is it that obvious?" she whispered, and without waiting for an answer, she swished off.

When the waitress was out of earshot, my mother leaned across the table and widened her eyes. "Oh my God, that's a man," she whispered.

"I know," I whispered back. It was obvious.

"I don't think she's had the surgery, though, do you?"

My mother loved watching surgeries on TV. She'd settle for gastric bypasses, but sex-change operations were her favorite.

She started riffling through her purse. I knew before she found it that she was looking for her lipstick. My mother was excited, and there was just something about the act of moving the stick of color across her lips that soothed her.

"I have way too much crap in this bag," she complained.

"Don't you just hate that?" the waitress said.

Neither one of us had noticed, but she'd returned and was filling up our water glasses. When she was done, she put the pitcher down.

"By the way," she said, turning toward my mother, "I love the cool way you do your makeup." She cocked her head and held her hands up like a picture frame. "It really works."

For the first time since the fitful application of her makeup, I realized my mother's face was a total mess. Misshapen ovals of rouge floated unevenly on her cheeks and her mascara was all over the place. She'd missed the outline of her lips with her lipstick, so it seemed as if she had two sets instead of one. She looked like a bad Picasso painting, and in my opinion, even his good ones sucked.

The waitress stood waiting for my mother to respond. The

two of them looked as if they'd just come off the same vaudeville act. My mother sat speechless. She still wasn't sure what to make of her.

"Goodness," the waitress finally said, clutching her chest. "Where are my manners?" She wiped her big hand on her apron and extended it toward us. "Allow me to introduce myself." Daintily and limply, she shook my hand first. "I'm Peter, but my stage name is Pam," she said in one breath as if the entire string of words was her name. "Most people just call me Peter Pam, though. It's less confusing. But on my day off," she continued, "I don't care what you call me, just don't call me early!" She guffawed, tossed her head back with a flourish, and when she brushed the hair off her shoulder, her wig rotated. She moved it casually back into place as if it were an integral part of the gesture.

"Anyway, what can I get you ladies?" She tapped her pencil on her pad, all ready for the order.

My mother was lost in the menu. Her eyes widened and my stomach ached as we scanned the pictures of food—pink and runny burgers, crispy golden french fries, mouth-watering, moist-looking turkey with gravy. I smacked my lips. When I saw the chicken "Fried to a Crisp in Top Secret Batter!" I moaned.

Then, abruptly, my mother snapped the menu closed, looked up at the waitress, and proclaimed, "We're going to split a blueberry muffin." I glanced at her pleadingly. It wasn't nearly enough. But I could tell by the way she looked back at me that right now it was all we were getting.

"That's it?" Peter Pam said. "That's easy. I don't even have to write that down." She stuffed the pad and pencil into her apron, turned in her yacht-size mules, and walked off.

When she came back, Peter Pam put the plate down with the bill next to it. Then from her apron pocket she pulled out a bag of chips, tore it open, and ate them standing up in front of us, chatting through each bite.

"My biggest dream is to play Agnes in *Agnes of God* on Broadway," she said, sticking a chip in her mouth.

"Oh my God," I said, "did you see Meg Tilly in the movie?"

"Oh my God," she shrieked. "She was brilliant. She should have won the Oscar. Don't you think?"

She shifted her weight to one hip, then absentmindedly handed me a chip.

My mother was watching me. She had no idea what we were talking about, I could tell, and she hated when this happened. Her lips twisted disapprovingly.

"Come on, Ruthie." She glared at me and slapped two bills down on the table and got up. "We're going." With her purse trailing behind her, she pushed the door open and walked out.

Peter Pam looked dumbfounded.

"It's not you," I said, sliding out of the booth. "She has her period."

"Ohhhh, that explains it." She nodded as if this were a tediously familiar problem.

"I suppose you think that waitress cares about you?" my mother hissed as I slid into the car. She really didn't like me striking up conversations with strangers, and being broke gave her mood swings. Anything could set her off.

She was finally fixing her makeup in the visor mirror. "Well, let me tell you something," she said, snapping the visor up. She turned halfway around and started rummaging through the backseat. "She couldn't give two shits about you. Take this." She handed me a sweatshirt. "Put it on. The gas station is open. You know what to do."

"Not here," I pleaded.

"Oh, don't be such a baby."

I hated it when she called me that, and to prove I wasn't, I grabbed the sweatshirt, got out, and slammed the door.

CHAPTER FIVE

Hunger

My mother pulled the car up to the gas pump marked full service. I walked into the station. The same guy who had told the waitress to let us in was sitting behind the register. He was wearing a baseball cap and glasses attached to a cord around his neck. He took them off when he saw me.

He gave me the key to the bathroom when I asked for it and told me to leave it on the counter when I was done. I went around the building and waited.

When he went out to pump our gas, I walked back in and looked around. There was a magazine rack against the windows, two short aisles of food, and a refrigerator section on the back wall.

My mother got out of the car, stood in front of him, and began chatting. She had washed her hair that morning in a sink at Cumberland Farms. It was down now and she was running her fingers through it, all animated and laughing.

He had his back to me, but I could tell he was really enjoying her. Not in a gross sort of way, because even though whatever my mother was saying was probably made-up and stupid, he considered her seriously—the way a father who had a daughter would. Which got me thinking about my own father and how I didn't have one, and then I thought about my grandfather and how I didn't have one of those either because my mother didn't have a father herself. There just weren't any fathers, grand or otherwise, anywhere.

My mother said she didn't know who my father was. Every time I asked about him she shut me up and told me he didn't matter. If I asked again, she'd shout, "I don't know! It could have been one of three or maybe four different men." But when I was little I had a clear picture of him. He had long hair with a crown of thorns circling his head. He wore blue tights with a red cape. He was Superman and Jesus combined. Sometimes when I looked up, I'd see him in the sky. Then, *shazam*, he'd land right in front of me. He'd smile a broad smile with teeth so white, one of them—*ting!*—sparkled and a ray of light would shoot up.

My mother tossed her head back, laughed at something the man said, turned slightly, and for a split second caught my eye. I don't know how, but she knew I was standing there watching them. The look she gave me was complicated. It was sharp-edged and pleading all at once.

So I did what I knew she wanted me to. I moved fast. I turned and went down the aisle behind me and saw my favorite snack, Hostess powdered-sugar Donettes—I couldn't believe they had them! I grabbed as many packages as I could and stuffed them under my sweatshirt. Because they tasted so much better with Diet Coke, I reached into the cooler behind me and stuck two cans down my pants.

I left the bathroom key on the counter and by the time I

made my way back to the car, the guy had finished pumping our gas and was now checking the oil. My mother was still blocking his view and chatting.

The cellophane crinkled when I slid back into the seat. The Cokes down my pants made it impossible for me to sit properly, so I propped myself up like a mummy.

The hood slammed down. "She's all set and ready to go," the man said, patting the car like a pet. He walked around and opened the door for my mother. When my mother got in, he closed it.

"Thank you so much," my mother said sweetly. Then she opened her purse on her lap.

"Well, let's see here . . . I have some money in here somewhere." I knew she was just stalling because the only time my mother knew exactly where our money was was when we were almost out.

My mother shook the bag and handed him some change.

"There should be at least a dollar there, and . . . let's see," she repeated, "I know my wallet is in here somewhere . . ." even though she didn't have one.

Meanwhile I was holding my breath trying hard not to move. My neck pinched and my shoulders ached. One of the Cokes was inching out of my pants. My stomach was totally frozen, and it was throwing my whole system off. My heart began to beat fast and the pressure on my bladder made me feel as if I had to pee even though I didn't.

"Here we go," my mother finally said, pulling out the last of our five-dollar bills and reluctantly handing it over. "That should cover it."

From the angle I was sitting, I couldn't see much of the guy.

The sleeves on his blue work shirt were rolled up halfway. A sprig of curly graying chest hair spilled over at the top button. His hands—rough and permanently dirty—looked like they'd worked hard all his life. He wore a wedding ring that I could just tell he never took off. There was an oval patch on the right side of his shirt with his name, Mel, sewn on it. The patch on his left asked, HOW CAN I HELP YOU TODAY?

Mel counted the bills; a single, a twenty, and a five. I watched them in the window as they passed through his hands. And when he came to the last one he hesitated.

"You know what?" he said. "Here, the oil is on me," and he handed my mother back the five.

"Oh, don't be silly." She shooed it away limply, pretending not to want it.

"Nope, nope. I insist, you got a kid to feed."

Then, "No, really, I couldn't."

My mother would blow a man or rob a store, but she never just took a handout. That day, though, we were desperate. She refused the money a prerequisite number of times until she finally took it.

I was so relieved when the charade was over, but then Mel took his glasses off and leaned into the car.

"You be good to your mother," he instructed, looking right at me.

"I will," I chimed, tilting my head, glancing at him, trying hard to act normal.

My mother started the car. When she pulled away I exhaled. I took the packages out and let the Cokes fall. I turned and looked out the back window.

Peter Pam was now standing under the bright white lights of

the gas station next to Mel. As my mother stepped on the gas and pulled out onto the street, the two of them waved good-bye to us like parents.

✧

The Diet Cokes rolled around on the floor and clanged together when they collided. The little bit of blueberry muffin we had at the diner only made our hunger worse. We drove just far enough for the lights of the restaurant to fade behind us before we veered off the road and abruptly stopped. My stomach growled, my hands shook, and when I handed my mother a package of Donettes, I fumbled it and it fell to the floor. For a moment it felt as if we'd never eat again.

"For Chrissake," my mother said as she reached down, grabbed two packages, and handed me one. I tore at the cellophane and yanked at the seam. Lack of food had left me weak and I couldn't open it.

I looked at my mother to see how she was managing. "Fuuuuck," she wailed, thrashing at her package as if she was drowning.

When we were hungry, we acted like savages. We'd take whatever was around—cake, cookies, a half-eaten slice of pizza picked right out of someone's garbage, it didn't matter what or where we found it—and we'd shove it in our mouths at once.

We looked over at each other, our instincts kicked in, and we tore our packages apart with our teeth like wolves. We stuffed the Donettes in our mouths, our eyes locked as if watching each other doubled the pleasure of eating. We sighed a grateful moan and we washed it all down with Diet Coke.

With a dusting of powdered sugar on our mouths, we stared

out the window and digested our food in a stupor. The moon was full and swollen with a warm and yellow glow.

"Now what should we do?" I asked.

"I don't know. Keep going, I guess." For a while we just sat there staring into space. My mother lit a cigarette. Cigarettes were the one thing she never ran out of. They were more important than food. She sat back in her seat and smoked. The engine was off, but the headlights were still on and a million lazy bugs drifted around in the beams. Then the moon slipped behind a rise in the earth and the night darkened. My mother flipped the visor down to check herself in the mirror.

"Fuck," she breathed, with little oomph. For the first time since we left Phil's, she snapped the visor shut without fixing anything on her face.

"Okay," my mother sighed. "Let's do it." She took one last puff off her cigarette, then flicked the butt out the window. She sat forward and turned the key, turned it again, and yet again. But all the car could muster was a shallow, tiny click. Then with a loud *pop!* a smoky cloud hissed up from the hood and the whole car slumped as if the tires had deflated.

My mother got out and slammed her door. She whacked the car with her pocketbook. "Piece of shit," she said.

There was no other choice. We walked single file back the way we came. She took quick, fast steps in front of me, wobbling in her heels on the uneven shoulder of the road.

"You know what I'd like to do?" she yelled back at me. "I'd like to go and give the asshole who sold us that car a piece of my mind." Then after a while, "You know the creep was married? He had a picture of his wife on his desk."

"Who would marry him?" I said.

"Exactly!" She jerked her head and spit the word out so hard, she stumbled and broke her heel. "Fuuuck." She steadied herself on the guardrail.

Whenever one of my mother's heels broke she'd just break off the other one and wear the shoes as flats. She'd bang it off on the counter or pry it off with a knife. The only time I saw her swing an axe was at a shoe. This time, she stopped and smacked the second heel loose on the guardrail. Then, like Hercules, she gritted her teeth, tore the heel off, and with a grunt, hurled it into the woods.

Without her heels, she picked up the pace. Not a single car drove by. I looked down and watched my feet. As we walked through the dark patches between streetlights, my sneakers changed from bright red to black, then back again. I didn't notice, but my mother had slowed, and when she stopped, I banged right into her. She was huffing and puffing, holding on to the rail, and for the first time, I heard how bad her lungs were. They rattled when she breathed, as if hundreds of tiny bones had come loose inside her.

"I gotta rest," she wheezed. She sat on the guardrail and hung her head. When she caught her breath, she opened her bag, riffled through it, then pulled out her lipstick.

She twisted the tube up and slid it over her lips in slow motion. Then she popped the top back on, sighed, turned it upside down, and read the label on the bottom.

"Ruthie," she said.

"What?"

"I want you to remember this: Ravish Me Red, by Revlon. When I die, and they're fixing me up for the wake, I want you to make sure they use this color."

"Mom," I pleaded, "*stop*."

There should be lots of color, she'd told me many times about her funeral. And she wanted to be buried with a supersize Diet Coke and a bag of jelly donuts. "Make sure they're from Krispy Kreme." Her hair should be up—French twisted in the back with her tortoiseshell clip. Her outfit was left to me. A dress or a pair of nice jeans would do, "but do not, under any circumstances, bury me without heels."

She tossed her lipstick back into her bag, took out a cigarette, and started to smoke.

My mother could make smoking look like a vigorous workout, or like a long cold drink on a boiling hot day. It could make her seem angry or gleeful or bored and I could tell when she was really feeling those things or only faking them.

But whenever she reached the end of a cigarette, she always looked the same: as if the fairy godmother of smoking had descended, waved her magic wand, and set my mother dreamily afloat.

I stood in front of her and watched. Sitting underneath a streetlight, she looked like an actress smoking on a stage. She took her first drag and when she blew the smoke up, her shoulders dropped. On her second drag, she stretched her legs out.

"Ahh," she sighed.

"Can I have one?" I couldn't help but ask.

My mother stopped. She narrowed her eyes and looked at me.

I had never dared to ask before. Smoking was the only thing she felt strongly I should never do.

"If I ever catch you with a cigarette," she'd say, her features pinched, the tendons in her neck pulled tight, "I'll kill you." She'd grit her teeth with her eyes afire. "You hear me?" She'd get right up into my face. Then she'd suck in a lungful of smoke and blow it out. "It's a nasty habit. And they keep raising the fucking price."

I was anticipating some version of this speech, but this time it didn't come.

"Oh, what the fuck. Here, you're old enough." And she thrust her bag at me. "Smoke away. What do I care? We're probably going to die on the side of this fucking road anyway." She flicked her cigarette butt out onto the street.

I stood there for a minute clutching her bag with my mouth open.

"Go ahead. They're in there somewhere. Help yourself."

I opened the purse, looked in, and frantically tried to think of something that would cheer her up.

"Did you know," I said, pawing through her junk, "that Anne Frank addressed her diary 'Dear Kitty'?"

Anne Frank was another one of my heroes. One school year, every paper I wrote had something to do with her, until the teacher told me I had to write about something less dreary.

"What the fuck are you talking about?" my mother asked.

"I know, right? It's totally confusing. I mean, wouldn't you think she'd address her diary, 'Dear God, you asshole'?" I took a breath. My head was now halfway in the bag, still digging around for cigarettes.

"But then," I continued, not wanting to drop the topic—it wasn't often that my mother agreed with my viewpoints—"I realized this is exactly why the book is popular. It is a firsthand account of the fact that even if you're doomed you can still find inner happiness."

"I have no idea what you're talking about, and give me that

thing." She snatched her purse, pulled her cigarettes out, put two of them in her mouth and lit them both. Then she handed me one. "And sit down, for Chrissake, you're making me nervous."

I sat defeated. I took in a lungful of smoke and coughed it out.

"Life sucks and then you die." She inhaled and blew her smoke up. "That's all you need to know. And you know what else? I changed my mind about my funeral. I don't care anymore; just burn me and throw my ashes in a landfill."

I opened my mouth to speak, but she cut me off. "I mean it," she said. "I don't care."

My mother's hand shook as she raised her cigarette to her mouth.

"What about your heels?" I asked.

"Pfft," she sneered. "You can burn them, too."

My mother had always believed that somehow, somewhere, there was a life out there that was better than the one we had—all she had to do was find it. But I had never seen her this low.

The streetlight above flickered, and, with a *buzz*, went out. The scenery around us went black. The only sign of life was the glow from the tips of our cigarettes as we smoked.

CHAPTER SIX

Humility

My mother grew up in foster care. She had a half brother but had no idea where he was or even if he was dead. She didn't know her father, and her mother died when she was six. If I ever asked her how, she wouldn't answer. Her eyes would glaze over, her cheeks would flush. After a while she'd pull me into her and say, "We got each other now, that's all that matters."

We had no other family—we moved too much to make friends. Besides, where we'd lived you had to watch your back with "friends." But no matter how torn and tattered or rough around the edges life could be, she was always there with me.

I swallowed and looked at her sitting on the guardrail, stooped and gazing down. Simple logic would never cheer my mother up. I knew her biggest weakness, though: she was squeamish. So I did the only thing that always worked: I rattled off all the most disgusting ways in which our lives could be worse. "We could have flesh-eating bacteria and uncontrollable diarrhea. We could have flesh-eating bacteria, uncontrollable diarrhea, *and* tapeworm. We could have flesh-eating bacteria, uncontrollable diarrhea, tapeworm, *and* elephantiasis."

"Stop!" she finally said. "Okay, okay, let's just keep going."

By the time we made it back to Tiny's, the restaurant was dark. But the bare bulb hanging just inside the gas station still glowed. Mel was there, sitting behind the register reading his paper. He folded the two halves together, then turned the page.

My mother pulled her brush out and ran it through her hair. She bent over and fluffed it upside down. She tossed her head back and when she shook it, her hair bounced in paisley swirls, then settled gently on her shoulders.

"Do I look okay?" she tilted her face in my direction.

A smudge above her eye went all across her forehead.

I stuck my hand in my pocket. "Here." I pulled out a napkin and wiped it off.

"Anything else?" She moved closer. "Look carefully." She turned her head side to side and presented each cheek to me. So I wrapped the napkin around my finger and blended in her rouge. Then I traced her mouth and tidied up her lipstick.

"There," I said. "You're perfect."

She sighed a half smile. "No, really."

"You look gorgeous, Mom."

"*Oh, please.*"

"You do. You look like an actress." She loved it when I said that.

"You really think so?"

It was true. Like in the movies, she looked beautiful, no matter how bad the lighting was.

"Totally."

My mother shrugged a shoulder, batted her eyes, and, as if to prove my point, gave a bashful little smile just like Meryl Streep would.

A breeze moved through the trees. A fragment of the moon dimpled the cloud above us. My mother pulled her tube top up and expelled one quick breath. "Okay, then," she said, "let's go." With her head held high she took center stage and strutted across the parking lot.

Mel saw us coming. He pulled his glasses off, put his paper down, and stepped out from behind the register.

With me behind her, my mother marched right in, slapped our last five-dollar bill down on the counter, and started talking. She went on and on, the whole story tumbling out about how she'd distracted him and I had only pretended I needed to go to the bathroom. "But we were hungry," she said, "and I don't know if you've ever been hungry, but it can be blinding. And now my car won't start."

There was a rip at the seam of her tube top held together by safety pins. There was a knot in the back of her hair that she'd missed. But she looked Mel in the eyes and she didn't sound fake. She sounded like herself—strong and human and not ashamed of anything. This was who she really was, but she almost never showed it. "Keep your guard up," she always told me. "Life, at any moment, will knock you down and kick you in the teeth."

"Please," my mother said. "I don't have much, but I'm a real hard worker, and so is she." My mother grabbed me and pulled me forward.

Superheroes, I realized, don't fly or look like Jesus. They drive used Fords like my mother's and they take their kids with them no matter where they go.

I took my hands out of my jean pockets, pushed my glasses up my nose, stood up straight, and smiled. Mel's eyes shifted and when he saw me grinning, a piece of him softened.

"You got any waitressing experience?" he asked.

Part Two

Part Two

CHAPTER SEVEN

Work

It turned out that Peter Pam was Mel's nephew and she lived in the apartment above the restaurant with Dave. It took us a while to figure out that Dave was not a man but a cat who wore a pink bow at an angle on his head. And Peter Pam spoke Yiddish because her stage character was Jewish, but Peter, the man, was not.

And Mel was not a father after all. "He couldn't have kids," Peter Pam whispered, sipping coffee.

We'd spent the night in the car and returned that morning. To help get us back on our feet, Mel was letting my mother work the breakfast shift and he was paying me to wash the dishes. He was giving us a kitchen tour, standing right in front of us, boasting about his grill, but that didn't keep Peter Pam from talking about him.

She leaned in, holding her coffee mug, pinkie extended. "They couldn't conceive because of Svetlana's *accident*." She stood up, raised her eyebrows, and nodded.

"Who?" I asked.

Horrified, she drew her hand to her chest and gasped, "Oh my God, nobody's told you about Svetlana yet?" as if we'd been working there for months.

"This here's an old dinosaur," Mel said about his grill, "but it still fires up every day." He patted the beast, grease-stained and charred, then showed us how to light it. "It's a beauty of a flame, isn't it?"

Mel was short and barrel-chested. His fingers were thick and his hands looked as if they could open any jar of pickles or peaches you brought him. His glasses had square plastic frames, the kind that were once in fashion, then went out of fashion, and even though they were back in fashion, on Mel they just looked outdated. He had a sad look in his eyes that never went away, even when he smiled. The roll of fat at the back of his head was deep enough to fit a nickel, and, except for a ring of salt-and-pepper hair, he was bald.

He stepped over to the fire extinguisher hanging on the wall and strained to reach it. "There we go," he said, finally getting it down. Then he pulled a handkerchief out from his back pocket and, without unfolding it, dabbed at his brow. "This here is how it works: you pull the pin out, and you pull this hose out and aim at the fire . . ."

"He's always overexplaining things," Peter Pam said. "Hey, Unc!" She put her mug down. "You're losing your audience here," and she presented us to him with her palms up the way Vanna White does with letters.

"Oh, yeah, well, you get the idea," he said, and moved on to the walk-in refrigerator.

Svetlana, we finally found out, was Mel's wife. "Let me tell you something, honeys," Peter Pam warned. "She was always a bit of a drama queen, but since the quote-unquote *accident*"—she paused to make air quotes—"left her in a wheelchair, she's a total bitch. The last thing you ever want to do is try to speak to her."

Suddenly, Mel stepped out of the refrigerator. "Well, that's the fridge," he said. "And that's everything you need to know about the kitchen." He wiped his hands together, *all finished,* and with his glasses still fogged up he pushed open the screen door and walked out.

A few minutes later at seven thirty sharp, the door opened again. A rectangle of light rolled out onto the floor and a woman stepped in.

"Don't listen to a word this knucklehead tells you," she said to my mother and me, pointing at Peter Pam. She put her travel mug of coffee down on the counter and walked directly to Peter Pam. "Come here, you big lug." She pulled Peter Pam down into the crook of her elbow and gave her a noogie. As if she'd been trained exactly what to do, Peter Pam closed her eyes and lowered her head. The back-and-forth slide of her wig was audible.

The woman then pushed Peter Pam to the side and took a bold step in our direction.

"Arlene here." She introduced herself with one big shake of the hand for each of us. "Mel told me to expect you."

A long hard life was embedded in the fine netting of wrinkles that traversed Arlene's face. A scribble of wiry orange hair buzzed about her head. Her eyebrows were penciled in to match. Her forehead sloped directly into the wedge of her nose. Her cheekbones, high and chiseled, were streaked with burnt-orange rouge and her fingernails were bright red. Tall, thin, and all angles, she was like a piece of furniture refinished and stained to look more expensive than it was.

"I'm the head waitress around here. If you got something to ask, I'm the one with the answers." She pointed and shook her thumb at herself. "And just so you know, I run a tight ship, so you girls better be prepared to work hard." She stood there and glared, baring her teeth just enough to scare us. But then her face softened. "Ah-ha, ha, ha . . . I got ya!" She tossed her head, exposing her missing back molars. "The last thing we do around here is work hard!" she howled. "You should have seen the look on your faces!" Her laughter abruptly became wheezing and the wheezing turned into a phlegmy cough and before long she was doubled over.

Then, suddenly, she stood erect. Her smile was gone and her face was bright red. Her forehead glistened with sweat and her hair looked as if it was on fire.

"She's having a hot flash!" Peter Pam declared. "Stand back!" As if she was saving us from a car accident, she threw her arm up and rammed us up against the counter. Arlene narrowly missed us as she stormed by and flung herself into the walk-in refrigerator.

"Thank God I'm not there yet," Peter Pam sighed.

That first day was a Sunday. The breakfast rush after church was about to begin. I stood at the sink in the ready position like I was waiting for a tennis ball to be served.

Washing dishes was my specialty. I'd worked this job before—at taco joints and Chinese restaurants back in California. I looked older than my age and I'd hustled for work every chance

I got. A good dishwasher, I knew, was always hard to find. My policy was that no dish would sit in my sink for more than a second before it got washed, dried, and put away. And all my pots and pans were always spotless.

Mel was greasing up the grill. He wore his baseball cap backwards. TINY's was stitched in an arc over the bill. When he left the kitchen to pump gas, he'd take his apron off and rotate the cap forward. I'd seen him do that twice already.

"Hey," he said behind me, "I almost forgot . . ." He pulled out an identical cap from his back pocket, punched it open, and curled up the bill. "Here," he tossed it to me. "It's an extra. I found it in my office."

"Thanks." I started to put it on.

"It goes backwards," he instructed, "and loosen up your shoulders." He rotated his own to show me. I twisted my cap, took a deep breath, and let my shoulders drop.

"That's it," he said.

A hand reached through the service window and slapped down the first order. Mel sprang into action. He shoved his glasses on, picked up the order, read it, took his glasses off, and swung them behind him on their string. He clipped the order to the bar above the counter and never referred to it again. He cooked up some home fries, grilled a pound of bacon, cracked a bunch of eggs, and made three complicated omelets faster than any cook I'd ever seen. Once in a while he tossed his spatula up in the air. Catching it by the handle, he'd sling it on the grill like he was playing a set of drums.

He finished the order and tossed the last plate down on the counter. "Order up!" he yelled with operatic bravado. Nobody heard him, so he whistled. A blunt, sharp note shot out through the space between his two front teeth and sliced the air in two.

"It's in his blood," Peter Pam remarked when she caught me staring at Mel as he scraped down the grill with long, graceful strokes. "His father was a cook and his granddad cooked for the army, the Pancho Villa War down in Texas. Lugged all his gear around on a mule."

"Order up!" Mel yelled again. Peter Pam picked up her order and disappeared through the door.

The back wall of the kitchen was lined floor to ceiling with shelves stocked with jars and bottles of ketchup, mustard, mayonnaise, and can after can of food—tomato sauce, black beans, pickles, and corn. Under the service window there was a butcher-block counter scarred with shallow knife-width impressions. Pots and pans hung down all over the ceiling and the space was so small, two people couldn't pass without one stepping aside. But Mel and I moved around each other like players on a court. When I cut behind him at the counter, he just knew to lean forward and let me by. It was amazing how well we worked together.

At the end of the shift, he wadded up his apron. "I tell you one thing," he said, "you got some serious talent. I never met a dishwasher as good as you." Then he pitched his apron into the laundry basket like a pro. And I beamed back at him.

Mel let us work again the next night and at the end of it, Arlene walked into the kitchen with a bottle of wine. She set it down on the counter and fished her corkscrew out of her apron pocket. After twisting it in like a pro, she stuck the bottle of wine between her knees. With a loud pop, her upper body spasmed and her arm flew back with the cork on the end of the screw.

"You're not a bad waitress," she said, raising her chin toward my mother.

We'd lied about my mother's waitressing experience. Besides her job at Donut Star, she didn't have any. But that didn't matter. My mother was smart, her instincts as honed as a fox's. She'd watched Arlene's every move and copied them exactly.

Arlene unscrewed the cork, snapped the corkscrew closed, and shoved it back into her apron. She reached underneath the counter, pulled out two wineglasses, filled them to the top, and held one out for my mother. My mother hesitated. She trusted no one. *And you shouldn't either.*

"What's the matter?" Arlene lifted the glass closer. "You look like a Cheshire cat just caught your tail," she said, completely botching the metaphor.

Arlene waited there grinning until my mother took the glass.

CHAPTER EIGHT

Trust

It was late by the time my mother and I made it back to the car. Before she settled in her seat, she stretched her leg, reached into her front pocket, and pulled out her tips. A cigarette dangled from her bottom lip. She squinted through a line of smoke as she counted the bills.

"Where's yours?" she said, glancing up briefly at me. "Fork it over." She gestured with her fingers.

I pulled out what Mel had paid me. She took my ball of wrinkled bills and flattened them out on her thigh. "I figured we need about six hundred bucks before we can fix the car and get out of here. We'll make it the rest of the way to Boston if it's the last thing I do. One thing I know for sure: *you are going to college*. With your brains they'll be lining up to give you a scholarship. Besides, I don't trust those people back there, especially that Arlene."

"She seemed nice," I said.

"Pfft," she went. "Those are the ones who turn out to be the biggest assholes." She flicked her cigarette out the window.

"You don't know that." In her whole life, she'd never given anyone a chance.

"What do you mean, I don't know that? Everyone knows that. It's a universal truth, like 'Shit happens' and 'Life is just one damn thing after another.' Those are not just stupid sayings, you know. Real geniuses came up with them."

"Geniuses usually end up killing themselves, which is like walking out of a movie before it's over, and everyone knows the ending can make a whole story fall into place."

My mother looked confused, but then her face brightened. "You see," she said, raising her eyebrows, "right there." She pointed at me smugly. "That's exactly what I'm talking about. I couldn't even follow that, that's how brilliant it was."

A shadow moved across the dark sky as my mother finished counting our money. In the distance, a possum paused beneath the streetlight. Its tiny little eyes glowed when it looked in our direction. Then it vanished into the woods.

"Wait a minute, that can't be right," my mother said. "Turn the light on." She nodded toward the dome light on the ceiling.

She re-counted the bills out loud. "A hundred and fifty. That's pretty good."

"Add that to the hundred we made yesterday and we've made two fifty already," I said.

She turned to me. "Oh my God. You're right." My mother never thought beyond the present day, so my math astonished her.

She counted the money a third time and was still musing to herself when my eyes began to close. She took a breath and finally noticed I was nodding off. She reached over, reclined my seat, then ran her hand across my bangs and kissed me gently on the forehead.

The next morning, I woke up with a start. The car was moving. We were going backwards at an angle. I gripped the dashboard and glanced over at my mother. She looked carsick. Her face was white. She sat upright in her seat.

We were being towed.

"What if they don't know we're in here?" I asked.

The thought sent my mother into panic. She leaned on the horn. I reached over and helped her.

In the movie of my life, she and I live fast and hard and when we die, we die together. Like Thelma and Louise sailing off a cliff. Or Bonnie and Clyde, gunned down as we run across a parking lot. But I never imagined we'd go like this. Not in a fiery car crash or a shoot-out, but in one anticlimactic act in a dingy scrap yard where we'd be crushed to death in our Ford.

Abruptly the truck pulled off the road and stopped. We backed off the horn. A shower of dirt pinged across the hood and a cloud of dust drifted through the windows. Then the car began to lower. It bounced when the tires finally hit the ground.

Footsteps headed in my direction. My door creaked open. Sunlight filled the car and gave the dust a blinding glare.

The air slowly cleared, and when I saw Mel standing there, the bill of his cap grazed with dirt, I knew our luck had changed. I could feel it in my bones.

"Life is shit." "We're all fucked." "People are assholes." These were a few more of my mother's favorite sayings. But Mel was kind to us. He didn't look at my mother the way men usually did. Instead he offered her a job. And me—he said he'd hire me any day of the week. I was so good at washing dishes, he gave me a dollar raise on the spot.

My mother didn't trust him at first. But then he replaced our battery and hardly charged us. And for fifty bucks a week, he rented us a room. It was a small space in the back of the gas station but it had everything we needed: a bed, a bathroom, and a microwave.

A whole week passed. He went on respecting her and being nice to me. And except for the occasional shove she might give you on her way to the refrigerator with a hot flash, Arlene was good to work for.

The river that ran through Fat River wasn't really fat anymore. It was more of a thinnish stream. Along its bank, in an old mill building, a company had once manufactured metal fasteners: screws, bolts, nuts and rivets. It employed the whole town. Crumbs and curlicues of extruded metal could still be found lodged in the crevices of sidewalks and between bricks. But the building that used to house the factory now sat deserted. It groaned when it was cold and sighed when it was hot, and sometimes it heaved and tossed a piece of itself into the dwindling creek. Peter Pam told us that people used to gather on the bank to see what had been lost of it, but now the building just slowly fell apart on its own.

In the nineties, Fat River tried and failed to reinvent itself as a tourist town. Tiny's, which was located less than two miles from the center on Route 6, was named after Tiny Irene. She had been one of the Munchkins standing in the crowd when Dorothy landed in Oz. But unless you watched the original, you wouldn't see her because she'd been cropped out when they resized the movie for TV. She was born in Fat River and even though she'd only lived there until she was five, no other place had claimed her, so the town of Fat River took her as its own. They erected a plaque in front of the house where she used to live and the merchants started selling T-shirts and coffee mugs with Tiny Irene's picture on them. According to Peter Pam, the design of these products was flawed. Nobody thought to pose her standing next to something for scale. "She just looked like a regular person. Nothing about her said, 'Munchkin,'" Peter Pam explained. So the souvenirs never sold. There were still some traces of Tiny Irene trinkets, but you had to look closely for them. They were pushed back on shelves, dusty and faded.

Seven years ago, a plastic tubing company set up shop fifty miles north of town, and last year, one town over, Walmart moved in.

Tiny's was made up of regular customers—people who lived in Fat River and worked at one of those companies. They came and left like clockwork. One guy, Bobby, worked for the town of Fat River. According to Arlene, this meant he did nothing. He did seem to be at Tiny's a lot.

Once, after the breakfast rush, I was stacking coffee mugs on the shelves below the counter. Arlene was leaning up against the wall behind me, filing her nails. Bobby was sitting in my mother's booth, still waiting for his food. He raised his empty coffee mug and signaled my mother for more. She grabbed the pot behind her, stepped around the counter, reached over his table, and poured him a cup. When she walked away, he tapped her on the ass and the *sh, sh, sh* of Arlene's emery board suddenly stopped. I turned around. She twisted her mouth and narrowed her eyes. She took her forefinger and thumb and pulled the sweat off her upper lip.

"Order up," Mel shouted. Arlene jammed her emery board into her apron pocket and pushed herself off the wall. It was my mother's order, Bobby's scrambled eggs and hash browns, but Arlene picked it up. She strolled out from behind the counter and in one perfectly orchestrated move, nudged my mother out of the way and tossed Bobby's plate down in front of him.

"Watch yourself, big boy," Arlene snarled. She was the first person I ever knew who could take down a grown man with a single short sentence. Bobby looked mortified, like he'd just peed his pants.

"Remember, I know your wife." Arlene had an on-again, off-again cheat for a husband. According to Peter Pam, Arlene had taken him back and kicked him out a thousand times over.

"And don't be so cheap with your tip, either." Arlene stuck her head in the air and pranced off.

"You don't need to take shit from anyone," Arlene had said to my mother. She lorded over the restaurant and protected her staff and I could tell it made my mother feel good. She sashayed away from Bobby's table, looked over her shoulder, and grinned at him all smug.

My mother couldn't help but like Arlene. They both smoked Camels and loved *Wheel of Fortune*. Mel had disappeared one day into the basement of Tiny's with Phil's old TV and emerged with it working better than ever. It now sat on the stainless-steel counter by the grill and every afternoon, Arlene and my mother would catch bits of the show while their customers waited.

And like my mother, Arlene wasn't afraid to tell anyone to fuck off if she had to. And she used that word almost more than my mother did. Arlene hawked the *k* out with a fierce staccato, infusing the word with sharpness. My mother pronounced *fuck* as if it were Yiddish—with a breathy, phlegmy, exasperated tone. *Fhhhhuuuuuuk.* The word itself seemed to bind them together. In no time, the two of them were standing, each with a knee bent against the wall, hissing a form of the word back and forth, using it to describe everything: the customers, the work, the weather.

"You can have the whole fucking lot," Arlene said to my mother about men. It was the last Friday in June. The restaurant was empty. My mother and Arlene were standing up against the wall. "I'm through with them!" When Arlene was off again with her husband like she currently was, complaining about men was her favorite thing to do.

Mel suddenly appeared from the kitchen without his base-ball cap, smelling of cologne, and Arlene stopped talking. She watched him leave through the front door and back out of his parking space. When his tailgate disappeared around the bend, Peter Pam burst headlong through the kitchen doors.

"I can't believe we almost forgot!" Arlene said.

And the two of them sprang into action.

Arlene pulled out a white tablecloth from under the counter and handed it to me. "Here. Go put that on the table by the window over there. And you," she said to my mother, "get some fresh bread and butter." Peter Pam walked around and spritzed the air with pine-scented air freshener. Arlene turned down the lights and set the music to smooth jazz. Everything was done in such a flurry, it took them a while to tell us what all the commotion was about: Svetlana was coming. Once a month, Mel picked her up and brought her back for an early dinner. And apparently she liked things just so.

It took twenty-three minutes for Mel to return with her. Arlene and Peter Pam knew this exactly because the minute before they arrived, we were instructed to put on clean aprons and stand behind the counter. Two seconds later, Mel pulled up to the restaurant.

Peter Pam and Arlene talked about Svetlana nonstop. Some of their most heated conversations were about her accident.

When Svetlana was young, she was an aspiring Olympic gymnast. But just before the trials she took a tumble down a flight of stairs and twisted her knee. According to Peter Pam, the injured knee sent her into a depression so deep that she threw herself in front of the truck on purpose. Her "*accident*" was no "*accident*" at all.

According to Arlene, she'd landed on her feet at the bottom of the stairs and a squirrel had caused the truck to swerve and hit her. As evidence, she'd cite the dead one they found plastered to the grill of the truck when they pulled it from the water where it had skidded off the bridge. But Peter Pam would point out there were no skid marks. They'd debate the time of day, the weather conditions, and the angle of the truck where it landed in the river, each building evidence to support their arguments.

The only thing Peter Pam and Arlene agreed about on the topic of Svetlana was that she was mean to Mel.

"He treats her like a queen and she barely looks at him," Arlene said.

"Mm-hm, that's right," Peter Pam nodded, as if this were church gospel.

"Why he hasn't wheeled her off and left her somewhere, I'll never know," Arlene continued.

But just watching him, I could tell that no one had a sense of duty quite like Mel.

He got out of his truck, walked around, and opened the passenger door. When he ducked into the car, I held my breath and watched as he lifted this mythical creature out.

Svetlana was much younger than Mel. She was small and delicate and looked weightless draped in his arms. With an air of grace and drama, her fuchsia scarf grazed the ground. Mel carried her across the parking lot as if he were her knight and she his Russian ballerina.

"Whatever you do, don't make eye contact with her, she hates that," Arlene whispered to us as Mel came through the door.

Mel gently placed Svetlana in the chair facing the window. He settled her at the table, unfolded her napkin, and spread it on her lap. Then he made his way to the kitchen, put his apron on, rotated his cap backwards, and cooked for her. When he was done, he sat with her and watched her eat. She didn't look at him and he didn't speak to her.

At the end of her meal, he carried her out, then lowered and placed her in the seat of his truck. And before he shut her door, he straightened her scarf and kissed her on the forehead. It was spellbinding to watch them together.

"I had no idea men like him existed, did you?" my mother whispered.

"No," I breathed.

"He's a good one," Peter Pam agreed, overhearing us.

"Why do all the bitchy girls get the nice guys?" Arlene asked, throwing her towel down and walking off. "For once in my life, I'd like to know."

CHAPTER NINE

Home

F at River wasn't much of a town. It had a hardware store, a gas station, a liquor store, and a bakery that was never open. It was not the sort of place my mother and I would ever live, but six weeks went by and my mother's tips remained good. Her jaw muscles relaxed and her shoulders dropped. For the first time in a long time she and I were saving money. In early August, when we discovered we had enough to rent our own place, my mother finally agreed to stay.

The only realtor in town, Frank O'Malley, worked and lived in a small space above the liquor store on Main Street. It was a Saturday when we drove to his office. We went to the back and up a flight of stairs like he told us to. My mother knocked on the door, but his TV was blaring and he couldn't hear us. She opened the door, stuck her head in, and yelled hello, but nothing happened, so we finally just went in.

The office was dark. A layer of dirt diffused the light from the skylight. A brownish hue languished in the air. His desk was large and oak. Two tattered old leather chairs sat at slight angles facing it.

My mother yelled hello again and the volume on the TV finally went down. A few minutes later, the wall of heavy curtains behind his desk parted and Frank O'Malley appeared.

"I didn't hear ya," he barked with an Irish accent.

He was a sturdy, graying redheaded man. Wires of hair sprouted off him in all directions, from his eyebrows, his ears, his temples. A fine tangle of red capillaries colonized the tip of his bulbous nose.

"I've just the place for ya," he said when we explained what we were looking for. "It'd suit ya right down to the ground. And I'd be obliged if ya took it off my hands."

He started going on about the owners and looking for the keys. The house, he explained, ducking behind his desk, checking all the drawers, was owned by the children of the family who originally owned it. Never a good thing, he stood up red-faced and told us. One of the siblings, he said, opening and closing drawers again, would call him and say they were going to sell it, then another would call and tell him, no they weren't. And it went on like that until he'd spoken to nearly all eight of them. As a result the house had been vacant for years. But our timing, he told us, was perfect. The family had taken a final vote, and for once a majority decided to keep it. Just last week, they'd put it up for rent.

Normally a long-winded story like this would bore me, but I could never resist the lilt of an Irish accent. And his was like music to my ears.

We had waited a lifetime for this. And here it was: me and my mother together making enough money to rent a decent place and pay our bills.

"Ah!" Frank O'Malley stood up with the keys in his hand. "I knew I had these bloody things in here somewhere."

The house was at the end of a dead-end in a cluster of prefabs and double-wides scattered like dice. Ours was the smallest on the street. A tiny one-bedroom built on a patch of earth that wasn't level, the house leaned a little to the left. The road wasn't paved either. It was gravel, and in some places, just dirt. There were overgrown shrubs under the windows and a pant leg of ivy grew up the trunk of an old oak out front. The house had light-blue aluminum siding so faded that parts of it looked white. But we fell in love with it right away. It was fully furnished. There was a couch to the left as you walked in, and to the right, in the front window, a table and two chairs. And there was a color TV at the foot of the bed, which was awesome because TV in bed was our favorite.

The sun was high and bright the day we moved in. The sky was clear and its color seemed deeper and richer than ever, like a million different blues mixed into one.

"After you, madame," my mother said at the front gate. She bowed and pantomimed me forward. We could not believe our luck. We'd arrived at a place called home, and we had gotten there together.

The gate was freestanding and wobbly. You had to pick it up on its hinges to open and close it. There was no fence attached; it would have been easy to walk around it. But on the day we moved in, we made a big deal about walking through it.

"Oh, no, please, after you," I insisted, mimicking her.

We went back and forth like that for a few minutes. I can't remember who finally entered first, but I do remember this:

The gate creaked and clicked when it closed and this seemed to set a whole world in motion. In the tree above, a mourning dove twittered away, leaves scattered, church bells rang in the distance.

"Yoo-hoo!" a voice called behind us.

When we turned, a woman was there, standing inside the gate as if she'd been lowered into place from above.

"Hi!" she chirped. "I'm Patti with an *i*."

Patti with an *i* looked to be around twenty-five. She wore tight jeans and a pair of red flats. Her eyes were heavily outlined with blue liner, and a high ponytail erupted from the top of her head in a celebration of hair, like fireworks. She stood in the middle of the walkway, holding a plateful of brownies on the palm of her hand like a waitress.

"I live over there with my husband and kids." She rotated with her plate, pointing kitty-corner across the street to a place that had all kinds of Big Wheels and scooters out front.

As she turned to face us again, the door to Patti's house flew open and a gaggle of kids—maybe three or four of them—spilled out. One of them ran across the street and plowed into her but she didn't seem to notice. She swayed like a pine tree and when she settled back down, her ponytail recovered to the top of her head. Somehow, she'd kept the platter of brownies perfectly still.

Another door across the street opened. Patti's next-door neighbor stepped out of her house. Behind her, a little dog jumped back and forth in the window, yapping at regular intervals.

"That's Pancake," Patti explained. "He's a six-pound Chihuahua who acts like he weighs eighty. If it wasn't for the funny look on his face, he might actually be frightening." Even from across the street, I could see the dog's pink tongue hanging out the side of his mouth.

"I can't say that about his owner, Miss Frankfurt. Now, she's scary."

I looked over at the woman descending her front steps. Wearing a beige housedress, she was set low to the ground and bottom heavy like a butternut squash.

"She's an ex-nun and the principal of Fat River High, and before that my English teacher. The whole town knows her as the Grammar Nazi. She'd flunk you if you didn't dot your *i*'s, which was how I got in the habit of dotting my *i* with a smiley face," Patti explained without taking a breath. "When we bought our house six months ago, I had no idea that she owned the one next door. Roger, my husband, says I'm obsessed with her. But he doesn't understand. He's not from this town. I feel like she's still watching my every move, just waiting to flunk me at something. I mean, it's like living next door to the pope."

Across the street, Miss Frankfurt minded her own business. She picked up her garden hose, opened the nozzle, and a shower fanned out in a perfect unbroken arc. Each drop crested and caught the light before falling with a patter onto her flower bed. When she was done, she grabbed her newspaper off her stoop and went back inside.

Patti took a breath.

A pair of yellow moths caught her eye; one landed on her brownies.

"Oh my God," she blurted as if surprised she still had them,

"I almost forgot. These are for you," and she handed the brownies to my mother. "They got a little burnt around the edges and the bottom, but the middle of them should be pretty good."

After that first batch of burnt brownies, Patti showed up almost daily with something equally inedible. At first she brought over whole things—a whole pie or tart—then she started bringing over pieces. And once she brought over just a few bites; a sad little pile of white frosting and cake. Before long, she just showed up empty-handed and she never knocked.

She'd stick her head in the door and yell, "Yoo-hoo?" as she let herself in. She usually came by first thing in the morning with her mug full of coffee. Initially we offered her a seat, but she always said, "Oh, no, I can't stay," and then that's exactly what she'd do. She'd stand at the door smoking and talking nonstop.

One morning we saw her heading our way. She'd slipped on Roger's work boots and was wearing one of his flannel shirts. Her pale yellow nightgown billowed out beneath it as she swooped across the street.

"Quick," my mother said as she locked our door, "in the bathroom."

Patti and Roger had just gotten a new set of binoculars from Walmart. "It's amazing how sharp they are," Patti had told us. She'd been using them to spy on Miss Frankfurt and every day she reported her findings in painstaking detail. "She eats cornflakes, without milk, for breakfast. She bends over and touches her toes every morning. She has a nightcap of whiskey before bed. She brushes her teeth up and down instead of sideways. Pancake sits on her lap when she reads. And she kneels at her bed every night when she prays." The details of Miss Frankfurt's life were endlessly boring.

"Yoo-hoo," Patti called as she approached our door. When she discovered it was locked, she rattled the knob. "It's me. Anyone home?" She knocked and pulled at the knob again. "Rita, Ruthie, are you in there?"

Then she started making her way around the house, peeking in all the windows.

Just before she got to the bathroom, my mother and I stepped into the shower stall. Through a crack in the shower curtain, I watched her. She reached up, cupped her hands, and tried to peer in, but a layer of dirt coated the window. She took her fingernail, scraped off a peephole, and shoved her eye up to it. It blinked and looked around.

Then she stepped back from the window and yelled, "Are you guys okay in there?" A moment passed. She pressed her ear to the peephole and listened. "If you guys are in there and you can hear me, don't panic! I'm calling the police!"

A minute later we relented. My mother barely opened the door. "Oh, thank God," Patti said, and wedged herself in. "I thought you were tied up in here or something. Didn't you hear me knocking?"

"Oh, we heard you all right," my mother said.

Patti cocked her head and looked at her, trying to decipher what this meant, but she couldn't quite make the leap.

"Well, anyway, thank God you're all right." Even though it was August, she stood there cupping her mug in a pair of pebbly gloves that didn't match. She had bad circulation in the morning, she'd told us.

I was making toast and my mother stood at the kitchen table

sorting through her stack of Crate and Barrel catalogs. She collected them and dog-eared almost every page.

"So, I gotta tell you guys something." Patti took a sip of coffee, put the mug down, and lit a cigarette, preparing herself for what promised to be another longwinded story. "So last night she was getting ready for bed. At first it was the same old routine. She brushed her teeth, she let her hair down. But then"—Patti took a drag off her cigarette, widened her eyes, and paused for effect—"after she knelt and said her prayers, she had trouble getting up. She gripped the edge of the mattress, but her hands slipped and she fell backwards! She had to crawl across the floor and hoist herself up on a chair. It was like watching a disabled crab. It was horrifying! I tried to get Roger to look but he just threatened to take the binoculars away. 'They're for the birds!' he shouted. But I can't help it." Patti raised a hand to the side of her mouth and whispered conspiratorially, "I mean she lives right next door."

She dropped her cigarette butt into her now-cold coffee. A single line of smoke rose up out of the mug with a sizzle. "Well," Patti sighed. She reached up, divided her ponytail in half, and pulled both sides to tighten it. "I better go check my laundry." Then she turned and walked out.

CHAPTER TEN

Kindness

Peter Pam wasn't much of a waitress. She dropped her trays all the time. She wobbled on her mules and her wig was always getting in the way, but I really liked her. She was smart and knew all sorts of interesting things. Like a cockroach can live for nine days without its head, a sneeze can exceed speeds of one hundred miles an hour, the oldest known vegetable is the pea, and ants never sleep. And we both agreed: the earth was burning up. Based on our assessment of this and many other things, we believed that God had traded his robe for a business suit and quit his job as savior for a more lucrative one, most likely in banking.

At the end of August, Peter Pam found me a bike in someone's trash. She was an expert at reusing and repurposing other people's garbage. It made her feel like she was doing something for the planet.

The bike was a bright-blue, three-speed Schwinn with a fender on the front and a rack on the back. It was on a Saturday morning when I first took it for a ride. No one was out so

I coasted down the hill in the center of the road toward Main Street. The air cooled my cheeks. I arched my back and spread my arms like wings. The wind fluttered the loose fabric down the sides of my T-shirt. For a split second, when I closed my eyes and rode with no hands, it felt like I was flying.

In my mother's lifetime, she'd worked at donut shops and nursing homes. She'd worked in retail and the fast-food industry, she'd cleaned rooms in hotels, been a cashier at a grocery store and a million different Walgreens. She almost never had just one job and not a single one of them ever paid enough, but here in Fat River we were breaking even. I had no idea what stability was until then. Life, it turned out, could open up and offer peace and space for friends.

Half of the stuff Peter Pam pulled from the trash was broken. And Mel could fix anything. He'd retreat into the basement with a broken motor and within minutes have it working. But the things that Peter Pam collected from the trash were beyond even his repair. Broken chairs and step stools, an old toaster oven, a baby carriage and various other items were piled behind Tiny's at the bottom of Peter Pam's apartment stairs. Once in a while she'd pick something up, an electric toothbrush, for example. "It's so wasteful," she'd sigh, examining it. "And look." She'd hold it up and rotate it for me to see. "It's perfectly good." Then she'd toss it back down in the heap.

What Peter Pam meant by "perfectly good" was anyone's guess because when I finally had to pedal, the chain fell off. I tried to fix it but it kept skipping, so I glided to an almost stop. I was on Main Street by then in front of Hanson's Hardware Store. The chain was rusty and needed greasing. I circled in the street debating whether to go in and buy a can of oil.

The owners of the hardware store, Dotty and Hank Hanson, were a frail elderly couple. They both used walkers with wheels on the front and tennis balls on the back, as if *thwack, thwack,* they'd lifted their walkers just in time to catch the balls there. Dotty and Hank stooped at the exact same angle. From a distance, the only way to tell them apart was by Hank's hat. He wore a black beret at an angle like an artist.

They lived right next door to us, "but you won't see them," Patti had said. According to her, they never went out and their hardware store was slowly going out of business. Whatever you were looking for, you could now find it cheaper at Walmart. Patti had warned us that Dotty now motored up and down her aisles looking for customers. "'Here, you need this,' she'll say, nabbing you and shoving some useless trinket—a key chain or screwdriver—in your hand."

The chain fell off again, so I stopped and parked the bike against their building. The mortar between the bricks was crumbling. The window display was a jumbled disarray of items. A hammer, partially buried under a blanket of spilled birdseed, sat next to an upright vacuum cleaner lying on the floor. There was a ladder leaning up against the window, a coffeemaker in one corner, and a screw gun in the other. It was like a Salvador Dalí painting I once saw in a book; no matter how hard I tried, it was impossible to build a cohesive narrative.

A distant chime sounded when I stepped in. The floorboards moaned. Fluorescent lights hung overhead. Half the bulbs were out. A haze of dust drifted in the air. A ceiling fan squeaked.

I managed to get what I needed and make it all the way up to the register without Dotty catching me.

Displays of impulse buys—mini hammers and screwdriver

sets, flashlights on goosenecks, magnetic retrieval tools, pocket-knives, mousetraps, dog whistles, fingernail clippers, Chapstick, an endless variety of key chains—were crammed on the counter. Racks of things for sale ran up and down the wall behind it.

Pinned above the register was a mishmash of warning signs: NO SMOKING, NO PETS, NO LOITERING, SHIRTS AND SHOES REQUIRED, and a sign that said BEWARE but didn't tell you of what.

I leaned over the counter looking for someone to ring me up. At first he blended in with all the stuff around him, but then I spotted Hank sleeping on a stool—his head down, his chin resting on his chest, his beret held loosely on his lap.

I cleared my throat once, then louder before he looked up and mumbled something. He gathered himself, replaced his hat on his head, hoisted himself up off the stool with his walker, then shuffled slowly to the register.

Without saying a single word, he picked up my can of oil, checked the price on the bottom, and put it down again. His hair was sparse and gray. A handful of rebellious coils sprang out from each eyebrow. The loose pockets of skin under his eyes pulled his face downward. He searched the register for the right numbers and when he couldn't find them, he lost track of what they were and had to check the price again.

In my peripheral vision, Dotty appeared. She maneuvered herself behind the counter with a clamor.

"For Chrissake, Hank!" she honked like a goose, "get out of my way." She nudged him with her walker. He fell back on his stool and almost lost his hat.

It was hard for me to imagine, but Patti swore that the Hansons used to be fun, and Arlene confirmed this. Apparently they used to come into Tiny's for early Sunday dinner every week, Dotty in her gloves and hat and Hank in a suit. They thought Peter Pam was a riot and, according to Arlene, Peter Pam knew it. She'd stand at the end of their table, doing all sorts of exaggerated things with her hips and hands, hamming it up for them on purpose. "You should have seen the way Dotty blushed and giggled like a schoolgirl," Arlene told us.

Without even looking at the merchandise, Dotty punched in some numbers, then grabbed a mini tape measure off a display and, without asking, charged me for it.

"It's half off!" she barked. She made it hard to feel sorry for her but I paid for it anyway.

When she handed me my shopping bag I grabbed it, but Dotty wouldn't let it go. I tugged a little, and she tugged back. I stopped and looked right at her.

Her scowl had completely disappeared. Her whole being had softened. She lowered her glasses down her nose and I saw in her eyes a well so deep you could never hope to see the bottom.

"You got my grandbaby's eyes," she said to me. "Hank, look. Don't she have Stephie's eyes?"

Peter Pam had told me the Hansons used to be religious. But they lost their faith years ago when an E. Coli–laden spinach salad killed their only granddaughter.

Hank got himself up again and the two of them looked at me as if I were their last morsel of food.

A shiver rose up my spine.

Dotty's grip loosened on the bag. I pulled it away and headed for the door.

"Wait," she said. "Please." I grabbed for the handle, but something stopped me. "I got something for you."

When I turned around, Dotty started rummaging through the shelf below the counter.

"Move it, Hank," she snapped, and down he went again on his stool. She gripped the edge of the counter. As her head went farther underneath it, her knuckles turned a pinkish white.

"Here," she exclaimed, triumphantly standing and holding up a small box. She took the box, shoved it into her apron, and shuffled around the counter with her walker.

"It's been sitting on the shelf for years," she explained, moving toward me. "It's probably antique by now." She reached into her apron and held the box out to me. For the first time, I noticed her name tag—MY NAME IS DOTTY. ASK ME FOR HELP—pinned on upside down.

"Go on." She nudged the box closer. "Open it, it's yours."

The box fit in the palm of my hand. The lid slid off easily. I moved aside some tissue paper, and nestled inside was an old brass bicycle bell. A mermaid was sculpted on top. As if she were perched on the bow of a ship, her hair blew back in an invisible wind. The sides were engraved with elaborate latticework patterns. The thumb handle was shaped like an oyster shell.

"You like it?" she asked.

"Yeah." I smiled. It was the coolest bell I'd ever seen. "Thank you."

"Hank!" she yelled over her shoulder. "Get over here with your screwdriver! Help her put it on and fix her chain while you're at it!"

CHAPTER ELEVEN

Resilience

Through the dense patch of woods behind our house, we could see the McDonald's on Route 6. The soothing scents of french fries and burgers wafted through the air and made us feel at home. But when the breeze of autumn set in and my mother registered me for school, the smells scattered and a cold dread replaced the summer's warmth.

"You're going to do great, honey." I had just turned fourteen and it was the day before my first day of high school. I was sitting on a stool in the bathroom while my mother cut my hair.

"When they find out how smart you are," she said, snipping away with the scissors, "I wouldn't be surprised if they let you skip ninth grade altogether. Yup," she said, nodding, "I can see it now. Yale and Harvard are both going to want you. I'm sure of it." She stepped back and lit a cigarette. "I was just thinking the other day," she continued. "You'd make an excellent president."

My political aspirations were meager to none. I did, however, have ongoing conversations with Hillary Clinton in my head.

She complained to me about Bill and she knew all about my mother.

My mother stepped back with the scissors limp in her hand. "Yup," she agreed with herself again, "with you as president"— she moved in and *clip, clip, clipped* at my hair—"there'd be no need for a vice one."

She kept starting and stopping and diving toward my head with the point of her scissors until she finally put them down. Propping her hand up with her elbow, she took a drag off her cigarette and examined her work. She tilted her head and blew the smoke out. Not quite finished, she rested the cigarette on the edge of the sink, pulled at my bangs, and clipped some more.

"And you know what else? . . . I think I make a damn good haircutter, don't you?" she asked, rotating me on the stool.

The haircut set the mood for the whole school year. It was unusually bad. My hair had been short to begin with but now it was way too short and it was totally uneven. I never told her, but for a week I wore a hat.

I hated every school I'd ever been to. Kids used to tease me for being plain looking, boyish, and poor. And my mother said I came into this world reading a book, so I'd worn glasses since I was five.

Fat River High was less than two miles from my house so I could avoid the bus and ride my bike there. But that was the only good thing about it. I wasn't afraid of much, but high school kids scared me. I was nervous and awkward around them and their behavior made no sense to me. The girls all acted stupid and the boys acted cocky and smart. When really you could tell just by looking at them that the opposite was true.

On my first day of school, it became immediately clear to me: avoid Sally Milander at all costs. In an instant, I could tell that she controlled the school. She left the boys awestruck, and when she moved down the hall a gaggle of girls traveled with her.

On my third day, I accidentally found myself standing behind her at the vending machine. The fleshy tops of her feet swelled in her rhinestone-studded heels. Encased in tight jeans, her ankles tapered up into a set of ample thighs. Her legs looked like sharply drawn *V*s making it difficult to imagine how she balanced on her feet.

When she bent to retrieve her bag of Cheez-Its, her hips bulged. Then she turned around, surprised to see me, and dropped the Cheez-Its on the floor.

Sally Milander was larger than life. From a distance her breasts ballooned out from the top of her tight shirts like pillowy rafts. But up close, they looked more like missiles. Her lips were pink and glossy, her eyelids rimmed with heavy black liner. And her brown eyes simmered. A reflection of myself dwarfed inside each one of them.

My face turned red and hot. I swallowed. "Sorry," I muttered as she glared at me.

When I went to pick up her Cheez-Its my glasses fell off. Before I stood up, she snatched the Cheez-Its from my hand. "Creep," she sneered, then kicked my glasses out of reach and walked away.

I had wanted to drop out of school way back when I first started at age five, but my mother kept me going. "I don't care what anyone says, you are going to do great things, and I don't want you to let anybody stop you."

I couldn't bear to disappoint her so I never told her how much I hated school. I felt around, found my glasses, put them on, bought my chips, and kept going.

CHAPTER TWELVE

Envy

In November a deep frost howled down from Canada and the cold settled in early. The leaves were still on the trees when the earth froze and the blades of grass twinkled with a coat of ice.

We had never experienced a winter before—we had no idea what we were in for. Even the onset of it was freezing. We bought ourselves down jackets and got into bed. Except for running back and forth to the bathroom, we barely used the rest of the house. And the TV at the foot of our bed was always on. Game shows, talk shows, classic movies, reruns, even infomercials enthralled us. McDonald's wrappers piled up on the floor. Islands of mold drifted in mugs of old coffee. When the temperature dipped at night, a thin layer of ice skinned the water in the toilet bowl.

One morning, my mother was getting ready to leave for work when she stopped and looked out the window. A delivery truck from Walmart had pulled up in front of Patti's.

"Pfft," my mother went when two oversize men lifted a La-Z-Boy out. "I hate those things."

Patti and Roger and all four of their children ate at Tiny's once a week. They always sat in my mother's section and even with her kids crawling all over her, Patti continued her tireless chitchat. She had moved on from obsessing about Miss Frankfurt and now talked nonstop about the redecorating they were doing. When they finished, the mess they left in and around their table was enormous. Ketchup and mustard on the walls, french fries on the floor, piles of sugar dumped out everywhere. And the tip they left was never big enough.

Three days later, around the same time, the truck was back at Patti's. This time, as my mother watched she lit a cigarette but didn't smoke it. She tapped it on the side of her ashtray, flicking the end of it with her thumb and waiting for the back doors of the truck to open.

"Oh my God!" she said as the delivery guys unloaded a couch. "It looks like leather." She watched dumbstruck as they maneuvered it up Patti's walkway.

Less than a week later on Veterans Day when we both had the day off, I was finishing a bowl of cornflakes and my mother was finishing her coffee. She stood up from the table, lifted her mug to take one last sip, but abruptly stopped. Another truck was barreling down our street. My mother lowered her mug slowly and fixed her eyes on the back of it like a dog fixes on a squirrel. She lit a cigarette, clenched her jaw, tightened her lips, and took short, clipped drags. When the same two guys emerged angling a flat-screen TV on their shoulders, she stabbed her cigarette out, snapping it in two. She flared her nostrils and two lines of smoke shot out.

"That's it. I've had it. Get your coat." Then she grabbed her bag off the back of her chair and walked out. The door banged shut behind her.

"Where are we going?" I struggled to find my sleeve, running after her.

She opened the car door and looked over the roof at me. "Where do you think we're going?" she said. "We're going to Walmart!" Then she pitched her purse over the driver's-side seat where it hit the back window, punctuating the air with a *smack*.

On a clear day in winter when the trees were bare, if you looked down Main Street, across the valley, and up the hill, you could just make out the giant blue *W* of the Walmart sign. It normally took twenty minutes to get there, but on that day my mother drove so fast it took us only twelve.

The automatic doors flew open and a jolt of white fluorescent light shocked us. My eyes slowly focused. The enormity of the place left me speechless. It was possible that one of everything in the world might be right here. The thought sent goose bumps up my arms. *My God*, I muttered to myself.

"Ruthie," I heard my mother say. "Ruthie," she repeated, shaking me. "Let's not get distracted. Come on, grab that." She pointed to a cart.

I took the cart and followed her. She turned left, she turned right, then I lost her briefly down an aisle.

"Look how cute this one is," she squealed when I found her. There were certain things my mother couldn't resist like T-shirts with cats on them. We had not made it far before she'd stumbled upon a whole rack.

The one she held up was hot pink and sleeveless. The Siamese cat on the front had real fake eyelashes and a collar studded with costume-jewelry pearls.

She turned it around, looked at it again. "I love it!" she proclaimed, then gleefully dropped it into our cart.

Before we knew it, we were roaming with no direction, filling up the cart with random stuff. We got lost in Kitchen Gadgets. There were so many of them! The musical cake slicer—"You'll never have to listen to anyone sing 'Happy Birthday' again!"— and the spork wizard, a battery-operated twirling spaghetti fork, were my favorites.

"What's this?" my mother asked, holding up a package.

I took it from her and examined it.

"It's a pepper mill," I declared, rolling my eyes. *How boring*.

"No, it's not." She took it back from me. "It's a flashlight."

I grabbed it back. "No, it's not."

"Yes, it is."

We passed the object back and forth, studying it like cave people would a phone.

"Oh my God," I finally said. "Look! It's both!" At the corner of the package was a small photo of a woman standing over her husband, peppering his salad in the dark, the "As Seen on TV" logo stamped beneath them in red.

"Oh my God, you're right," my mother said.

Enraptured by the possibility of this thing, we stood there holding it between us until my mother turned it over. "It's only two forty-nine!"

Oh my God, oh my God! We hyperventilated the phrase to each other, like a call-and-response hymn.

"Let's get it!" And even though we never peppered anything, let alone in the dark, my mother tossed it into our cart.

Less than halfway through the store, the cart was overloaded. A review was in order. "What the fuck do I need this for?" my mother asked, picking up a soap dish she'd loved just minutes ago. "It's hideous," she declared. She crammed it onto a Tupperware shelf miles away from where we'd found it. One item at a time she pulled stuff out of our cart, leaving a trail of crap lining the shelves in all the wrong places, only to replace each discarded item with a new one. In Walmart, time passed unnoticed. We got hungry and dehydrated. Delirium set in. The sharp fluorescent light cut right through my mother's temples and her headache flared up.

"We gotta get the fuck out of here," she said, abandoning the cart altogether. She was sweaty and agitated and needed a smoke but finding the exit proved impossible. The maze of aisles led nowhere. We doubled back through Bath and Bedding twice. We got stuck in Luggage. And then I lost her. I looked up and *poof,* she was gone.

I panicked. I imagined us as wandering Jews in the desert. We'd pass each other in adjacent aisles without knowing it. Disoriented and starving, we might easily collapse in Housewares just yards away from one another. To the sound of Muzak, in the cradle of Chinese plastic, our lives would fade to black and our story would end.

I looked across the store, and there, far away in the distance, I recognized my mother by the way she stood when she was looking up—with her head back, her shoulders down, and her hands in the back pockets of her jeans.

When I reached her, she sighed. "It's on sale."

I looked around and caught my breath. A canyon of flatscreen TVs loomed over us.

Live with Regis and Kelly was on and they were doing their thing: cackling together like imbeciles. Regis tossed his head back and laughed harder and Kelly smacked his knee and the antic repeated on every screen around us.

"We'll be right back," Regis managed to choke through his laughter.

"You get a fifty-dollar rebate if you charge it," I heard my mother mutter.

I was spellbound by a Scott paper-towel commercial. Apparently just owning a roll of it would give us a better life.

"Ruthie," my mother said, tugging on my arm. "Did you hear me?"

A wall of pepperoni pizza from Pizza Hut now glistened in every frame. A hunger pain roiled in my stomach.

"Maybe we could get a credit card and charge it," my mother said.

My mouth watered. I still worked the weekends and a few hours after school. Even with our dip in income, we were doing fine.

"Could we qualify?" I asked.

CHAPTER THIRTEEN

Winter

By early December it was frigid out. Our windows were drafty. The one in the kitchen was missing a pane. I sealed it with cardboard and plastic, but it didn't matter. The cold seeped in and the wind sliced right through our walls.

An Alfred Hitchcock marathon got us through until the middle of the month. *The Birds* was my mother's all-time favorite movie. To me, the final attack scene struck a false note. I simply could not believe Tippi Hedren's character could be so helpless. I wrote a whole paper on the topic for English class once. Despite my A-plus, my mother insisted the leading man had to save her. "It's the story of romantic love," she'd argue. She and I never agreed but it was the only intellectual debate we ever had, and we both felt smarter when we had it.

In the weeks before Christmas the Hansons taped elegant candle lights in their front windows. Miss Frankfurt hung a tasteful wreath. Pancake donned a string of bells that jingled daintily when she walked him.

But Patti and Roger were Christmas zealots. Their house was ablaze. The roofline dripped with bright red icicles. Their front yard was scattered with little plastic elves. A giant inflatable Santa rocked back and forth waving while Bing Crosby's "I'm Dreaming of a White Christmas" blared out from a speaker hidden in a bush blinking with gaudy blue lights.

For me the whole focus of Christmas was off. It was all Jesus this and Jesus that—not a single thing about Mary. I protested the holiday by acting as if it was hers. I outlined our door with my string of blinking Madonnas and I set up the rest of my collection on the front windowsill facing out.

The older my mother got, the more she hated Christmas. The lights gave her headaches and, as if a chorus of elves had infiltrated her brain, the Christmas carols kept her up at night sweating. "They won't stop!" she'd shriek, holding her temples.

Christmas was a celebration of money and we never had any. Every year we'd give each other the same gifts. I'd get her hair bands and nail files, little things that were easy to slip into my pocket at The Dollar Tree. And she'd give me socks. The lead-up to the holiday made her want to kill someone and the actual day made her want to kill herself. Last year, on Christmas she got into bed with a bottle of vodka. When she was good and drunk, she reached over the side, hauled her bag onto her lap, and fished out her lipstick. "Do me a favor, would you?" She fisted the tube in her hand and in a drunken scrawl the lipstick went all over her mouth. "Wake me up when this is over."

But that year in Fat River was different. Mel had given everyone a Christmas bonus. So on Christmas eve we turned up the heat, took our coats off, and lip-synched to Madonna all night.

Neither one of us could wait. Just before midnight we nestled all snug in our bed while visions of flat-screen TVs danced in our heads.

✧

"It's here!" my mother screamed the morning after Christmas. She raced around, hopping into her slippers, then she flew out the door. For the first time in our lives we'd qualified for a credit card, and our very own flat-screen TV had arrived.

It was so big, the delivery guys had to take it out of the box to get it inside the house. And no matter how many ways they angled it, they couldn't fit it through the bedroom door. So they set the TV up in front of the couch.

The couch was full of junk but with a swipe my mother cleared it onto the floor. It was late afternoon and *Jeopardy!* was on. We loved this show. We almost never knew the right answer; when we did, we screamed it, and the jolt of adrenaline we got kept us hooked.

"This is amazing," my mother said. We were drinking Diet Cokes and she was shoving fistfuls of chips in her mouth. She was wired from all the excitement. "You like it?"

"Yeah! It's great!" I sounded a bit overenthusiastic. In reality, I couldn't read the clues. The couch was too close to the TV, but there was no other place to put it. I didn't like watching television sitting up, and the high definition was so sharp that every bump and blemish visibly erupted through the makeup. It was gross.

A week went by. The radiation started giving us headaches. My mother went through a whole bottle of Advil. On the night that she ran out, she gave up. In the middle of *Cheers* (one of her favorites), she announced she was getting into bed to flip through her catalogs and I decided it was time for me to read a book.

For days we pretended not to miss seeing our shows. But then one night when we were in bed, my mother sighed and tossed her catalog onto the night table. She picked up the remote, and with an outdated buzz, our old TV was on again.

By mid-January, half the lights on Patti and Roger's bush had gone out and Santa was lying on the ground. The only thing that still inflated was his arm. It bounced up and down and every time it hit the ground, it shook back and forth twice.

By February, one of the kids had knocked over the speaker so Bing Crosby now crooned into the dirt. Santa was completely deflated but the plastic went on vibrating in the same *rat-tat-tat* pattern right through to the end of the month.

Then one night, around one o'clock in the morning, we heard a noise. We got out of bed, pried open the slats on the blinds and peered out. The sky was dark velvet and the scattering of stars were pins of jewels. Half the moon looked tucked inside a buttonhole. The other half cast long purple shadows in the light dusting of snow.

The sound was getting closer.

"Where's that coming from?" my mother asked. It was hard to tell.

"There," I said. "Look!"

Moving across our window frame from left to right, Hank was hunched over his walker. With one long *chshhhhhh* he pushed the walker forward on its tennis balls, and then with two shorter *shh, shh*s, he dragged himself behind it. He kept his head down and looked at his feet, astonished, it seemed, to see them move.

"What's he doing?" I asked.

"I think he's jogging."

"You can't jog with a walker," I said.

"Well, that's a jogging suit." I looked and realized she was right. He was wearing sneakers and a red velour sweat suit. Instead of his beret, a headband circled his head.

The streetlight cast a globe of yellow on the road. Hank shuffled across it. The little gray wisps of hair on the top of his head glowed. Then he stopped. He dabbed at his brow with his left sweatband. Then he gripped the walker and began to move again.

"Oh my God," my mother said. "Where is he going?"

He made a three-point turn to the left. Then he headed off the road onto Patti's yard. We watched him navigate around a Big Wheel and a hockey net. When he got to the bush he stopped.

"Oh my God, is he peeing?" my mother asked. Then, "Oh my God, he's on the ground!" We held our breath and covered our mouths. Hank was on his hands and knees. He might have needed help, but neither one of us moved for fear we'd miss what might happen next.

He began feeling around in front of him.

"He dropped something," I said.

"He wasn't carrying anything," my mother pointed out. "Oh my God, what's wrong with him?"

He now reared back like a horse. It took us a while to realize he was pulling at something, and then suddenly, it snapped. He fell backwards and in the instant just before he hit the ground, the Christmas lights on the bush stopped blinking, the air pump went off, and Bing Crosby finally croaked his last note. Hank lay on his back like a june bug, holding up the end of the plug.

CHAPTER FOURTEEN

Contentment

In late March, timid tongue tips of daffodils and crocuses poked through the surface of the ground and then—*bam!*—overnight they shot up and sprayed the earth with color.

At the end of May the Hansons took out a loan and threw a "Grand Reopening" party for their hardware store. Two men showed up with ladders and buckets of paint, whitewashed the storefront, and cleaned the windows. And at long last the window display changed. A wheelbarrow, a sprinkler, a weed whacker—there was now a decipherable garden theme. They replaced the mishmash of warning signs at the register with a tasteful photo of themselves, young and grinning, with the caption, "Proudly in business since 1950."

Together with a giant pair of scissors, they cut a red ribbon. For the first time since I'd known her, Dotty looked happy. She leaned over her walker, pinched Hank's cheek, and when she pecked him on the mouth, the crowd erupted.

In the parking lot, under a tent, a small band played. Tiny's provided the food—hamburgers, hot dogs, potato salad, Coke, wine and beer. As if on thrones, Dotty and Hank sat at the edge of their party in folding chairs. Gazing around and holding hands, they beamed.

✧

Something always happened to send us tumbling to the bottom. My mother would lose her job somehow—she'd get sick and they'd lay her off or just replace her. But it had been ten months, almost a year, since we'd been in Fat River. It was the longest we'd ever stayed in one place.

My mother eased into herself in a way I had never seen. She smiled and laughed more easily. She became more sure of who she was: smart, quick-witted, and clever. And she now appreciated things she'd never had time to. More than once I caught her marveling at the vastness of the sky. As for me? I stopped biting my nails, and for the first time in my life, I slept like a baby.

The good times were affecting everyone. Even Svetlana showed up for the party, and Svetlana never went out in public. Arlene claimed it was because she had agoraphobia. Peter Pam was sure the cause was OCD and anxiety. But the truth was people stared at her. Mel had pulled up in his truck with her and a crowd had already gathered. They hushed and parted as she wheeled by them.

Normally she'd just glare up at them and they'd scatter like Raid-blasted ants. But that day, she rode in on her chair as if it were a thoroughbred. A slight but discernible smile graced her lips.

Then I realized what was different. Her wheelchair was brand-new. Mel had been saving up for months. And here it finally was. A red, sleek, and shiny three-wheel scooter with six speeds and a basket. And Mel didn't have to push it. He walked beside her with a glow.

Svetlana's features were sculpted and fine. Her blonde hair was pulled back in a perfect French twist, and her almond-shaped eyes twinkled blue. She had just one Chardonnay but that was all it took. When the band struck up the tune to "Endless Love" by Lionel Richie, she put her glass down and shifted forward. She pulled out from under the tent and into the center of the parking lot. As if the gymnast inside her had sprung back to life, she started pirouetting in the gravel. A series of perfect figure eights reached a climax. Awe rippled through the crowd when she straightened the wheel, raised her arm, and steered with one hand. She tilted her head up and arched her back. When a cloud appeared and blocked out the sun, she took her red scarf off, trailed it behind her, and splashed the shadow with color.

It was grace like I'd never known it.

The next morning at work, Peter Pam and Arlene were still in disbelief. They'd never known Svetlana had that kind of unadulterated beauty inside her. "I mean, she always seemed like such a bitch." Arlene said.

"It is confusing," Peter Pam agreed.

Arlene glanced up with a slight smile. Her eyes twinkled as if she were reliving Svetlana's performance. "Oh," she sighed, throwing her dish towel down, "who cares how the accident happened. It's just a damn shame. And you know what else?" Before anyone could answer, she said, "I'm even thinking I might have her over for dinner someday, you know, get to know her a bit."

This, of course, would never happen, but the times were bringing out feelings in people they never knew they had before.

I will always remember that Sunday morning after the party. We were so busy debriefing about it that nobody noticed, but the sky outside had darkened. A gale of wind touched down so fast, the building shook and the dishes rattled.

Our chatting stopped and we moved to the window to look out. The rain would come any minute now. Another gust blew straight across the parking lot.

"Hey," Arlene said, untying her apron and slapping it down on the table. "Come with me." She reached down and took my wrist. "I gotta show you something. It's perfect weather for it."

And before I knew it, we were outside. The dusty wind howled and whipped around our heads. Tugging me along, she shouldered through to the middle of the parking lot, where she stopped. She squatted, thrust her face forward, and grinned so wide it turned her eyes to slits.

"You hear that?" she yelled over the wind.

"Hear what?" I asked.

"Come closer." She pulled me in. "And close your eyes." Then she assumed the same strange position, only she held it much longer.

The sky was beginning to spit. Any minute now it would pour, but I did what she told me. I closed my eyes and listened. And then I heard it. Above all the other sounds, a low, deep, smooth note emerged and hovered there. It was the tone of the wind whistling through Arlene's missing back teeth and it was beautiful.

"Oh my God, that's awesome!" I shouted.

"Isn't it?"

Arlene knew how to do all sorts of things. She could weave in and out of the kitchen and around her tables. Juggling dishes and glasses, cups and saucers, bowls and coffee mugs, like Sam I Am, she never dropped a single one. She could snap her gum to the tune of "Mary Had a Little Lamb" and she could twirl the bridge of her front teeth all the way around and put it back in place without opening her mouth—not even once.

"Oh please," she'd said to me, "that's nothing. When I was younger and my damn knees weren't so shot I could ride a unicycle." And the next day she showed me a picture to prove it. It was creased and faded but there she was, age twelve, her arms outstretched for balance, tall even then, perched atop a bright red seat, grinning from ear to ear.

The wind hushed and the tree branches swatted the clouds. A new jet stream of air rushed in and rain fell in buckets. Arlene and I stood together in the parking lot with our palms up.

The days that year had taken on a rhythm like they never had before. They had a leisurely ambient flow, the kind of flow that lowers your heart rate. Life was never perfect. But I remember on that day, it felt close.

CHAPTER FIFTEEN

Well-Being

At the end of July our realtor, Frank O'Malley, called us. One of the siblings had passed away and the family had taken another vote. They were selling the house.

My mother was sick over the news. She crawled into bed and stayed there, missing a full day of work. It was the first time we'd ever had a consistent place to live and I didn't know how badly she'd needed it until then.

Days went by with her like this, but early one Saturday morning, a black SUV pulled up in front of our house.

The car idled there while a man inside gathered some papers. The driver's-side door opened. A moment passed, then a pair of boots hit the ground. He wore a cowboy hat and a suit. Prosperity was visible in the crease of his pants. He stood there a minute, adjusted his hat, straightened the knot on his tie, and walked to our front door.

My mother and I answered his knock together. She was still in her slippers and robe. He filled the doorframe when we opened it. He held his hat in his hands. His hair was thick and dyed black. A visor of it swooped forward and shaded his eyes. The part down the side was perfectly straight, as if he'd used a ruler to make it. A marble could've fit in the dimple of his chin.

"Who the fuck are you?" my mother asked.

She didn't trust men in suits. "Stay away from them," she'd told me. "They're ruining the world."

My mother looked over his shoulder to see where he'd come from. Where there was one, there could be a whole army of them.

"Name's Vick Ward, and I'm not here to sell you anything." He smiled broadly. His teeth were so bright the spaces between them seemed spackled together.

"Yeah, right." My mother took a drag off her cigarette, blew it out the side of her mouth. "And I was born yesterday."

I chuckled, crossed my arms, shifted my weight to one hip, and stared at him, waiting for his response.

Salespeople made us feel smart. When they called, my mother would pretend to listen to their pitches but really she'd be covering the receiver and she and I would be laughing. Then finally she'd say, "Let me go get my wallet," but instead she'd hold out the phone and shout directly into the mouthpiece, "Fuck you, loser!" then slam it down. It was hysterical. It'd take us hours to stop howling.

"Well, now, if you give me just one minute of your time and hear what I'm about to tell you, I can guarantee it will make you very happy," Vick Ward claimed.

"I doubt it," I said.

For the first time, he looked at me. His grin widened. His crow's-feet deepened. "Well, aren't you cute." A barely discernible hint of sarcasm lingered in his voice.

"Don't call her cute," my mother said. "She doesn't like it." When she went to go close the door, he stuck his boot in it. The toe was shiny and black. My mother looked down. Intent on crushing it, she pulled the door harder, but Vick went right on talking.

"Did you know, a month after the people across the street bought their house it increased in value by ten thousand dollars? And you have better credit than they do. According to my records, you've never missed a credit-card payment."

"We haven't made one yet," I said. We'd gotten a no-interest, no-payment-for-a-year deal on the one we got at Walmart.

"Yes, indeed." He ignored me, his foot still in the door. "You are more than qualified to buy this lovely home. You don't need a down payment, you don't need a tax return, you don't even need a job!" He was almost gleeful.

"Didn't we just see you last night on an infomercial dicing onions?" I snickered and looked at my mother, thinking this would make her laugh. But she wasn't listening.

She'd stopped pulling the door closed and was staring across the street. Another delivery truck had pulled up to Patti's. The back doors swung wide open.

My mother took a long hard drag off her cigarette. She eased the door open, tossed the butt onto the stoop, stepped out, and crushed it with the ball of her slipper. She glared at Vick Ward, blew a line of smoke straight up.

"You got ID?" she asked.

✧

Behind our house, bolted down to a platform of overgrown cement, there were two lounge chairs that we'd thought were trash, but that summer we cleaned them up and discovered they were perfectly situated for a pool.

So we lay around as if at a hotel, gossiping and dreaming like girlfriends. And my mother laughed at all my jokes. We snapped our fingers and ordered drinks from an imaginary waiter who we agreed looked like Leonardo DiCaprio. "He's so cute!" she swooned.

One night late that summer after work, she was straddling her lounge chair counting her tips and complaining how things had slowed. Fewer people seemed to be eating out.

"It will pick up," I told her, sure of myself, sipping my Coke. Through a line of trees the lights from the McDonald's on Route 6 buzzed. Little bits of the yellow arches wove in and out through the shadowy branches. The breeze that night carried fragments of orders from the drive-thru. Individual words— *please*, *double*, *burger*, and *large*, drifted into our backyard and landed around us like paper airplanes.

"It's August," I explained. "People go on vacation. Most people take at least two weeks off. Therapists take the whole month!"

"Most people I know don't take a single day," my mother said.

"It's different now." Feeling cocky, I took another swig of my Coke.

For the first time in our lives, instead of falling further behind, my mother and I were moving up. That year it seemed as if the heavens had parted.

"We're not most people anymore," I reminded her. "We're homeowners. It's a guaranteed cushion if you fall."

At first we thought it was too good to be true, but Patti told us she never thought they could afford to buy a house either. And we looked it up: American Mortgage, where Vick worked, had been around for years. There was hardly any paperwork. All we needed was my mother's signature, and overnight we became queens and our little house became our castle. We spent hours dreaming how we'd fix it up. We could plant flowers in front, my mother said. And, oh, wouldn't a bird bath be nice. We'd fix the leak in the ceiling and replace the siding and how about if we painted the kitchen red?

"You know what?" my mother finally said. "You're right." She folded her dollar bills, sat back in her chair, and stuffed them into her pocket. "And you know what else?" She tapped me on the arm. "You and I need a vacation. Now, where do you think we should go?"

Paris, London, Rome. We looked at the sky and sighed at the thought of each one.

CHAPTER SIXTEEN

Hatred

Like a long, cool glass of water after hours of thirst, relief had finally come our way. A year went by. In school, I stopped caring what people thought of me. In my mind I saw myself as a star in a ticker-tape parade, perched on the back of a convertible waving to the masses. Sally Milander would see me on TV. I imagined her on her couch as I knew she would be: overweight, pregnant, and married to an asshole.

Then, sometime in early 2007, things began to shift. The plastic tubing company north of here moved its vacuum-hose production to China. A few months after that, medical tubing went and a gang of teenagers sprouted up on Main Street. They'd ride their skateboards up and down the middle of the road and when they got tired they stood around, kicking the earth and smoking.

One night just before closing, in June of that summer, two of the older ones came into Tiny's and settled into one of Peter Pam's booths.

One of them wore a red cap, the other had a shaved head and a tattoo—a tangle of snakes weaving up his arm. The one with the tattoo did all the talking; the other one just sat there. His blood-shot eyes roamed around and surveyed the place. My mother and Arlene were already in the back wiping off ketchup bottles.

When Peter Pam brought them their burgers, the one with the tattoos said something to her and the other one snickered. For a split second Peter Pam hesitated, like she wasn't certain how to take it, then her face softened. She said something—mocking and teasing them right back. And before I knew it, they were laughing like friends.

When they finished their burgers and got up, I was stacking coffee mugs behind the counter and Peter Pam was wiping down her tray.

"See ya later, doll," the one with the tattoo said to her as he walked by. Then just before he left, he turned, widened his eyes, and flicked his tongue in and out. A silver stud, pierced right through it, winked in the overhead light. His teeth were jagged and gray.

"That's gross," I said.

"Oh, please. That's nothing." Peter Pam pushed up on the bottom of her wig and lifted a hip like Marilyn Monroe. "They just know a good-looking girl when they see one."

Mel came out and locked the front door. He unplugged the neon chicken wing and the hot dog flashing in its bun, said good night, then left through the back.

When the four of us finished cleaning up, we slid into a booth—me and Peter Pam with our Diet Cokes, my mother and Arlene with their Chardonnays.

"Oh my God," Peter Pam said, "I'm exhausted." Then she unbuttoned her top button and started removing the stuffing from her bra: a wad of newspaper, toilet paper, and a few crum-pled-up restaurant orders spilled out.

Peter Pam refused to fill her bra with anything but recycled material. That's how much she cared about the earth. Her boobs were always uneven and lumpy and anything could be in there. If you accidentally brushed up against one you'd never know what kind of sound would come out. One day, as she clutched her tray to her chest, her left breast squeaked. "Cat toy," she'd explained when I looked up. "It was nice and round."

"Reduce, reuse, recycle," Peter Pam sang, taking a plastic sandwich baggie out of her left cup.

"Oh, please, not this again." Arlene rolled her eyes and took a swig of wine.

Arlene threw all her trash out on purpose just to aggravate Peter Pam and at the end of the night Peter Pam would dump the whole barrel upside down and fish out every tiny bit of plastic just to aggravate her back. They were like an old married couple in the way they loved each other but disagreed about everything.

In Peter Pam's vision of the world every living creature had its place. If she ever came across a spider or an ant, she'd walk it out, ease it off a magazine, and wistfully watch it go. But Arlene beat insects dead with a broom. And she was wild about it, letting out a string of hoots and howls.

"Oh, look," Peter Pam said, "a quarter!" as she pulled it out of her bra.

Arlene picked up her pack of cigarettes and smacked the bot-tom against the palm of her hand so that two of them stood out. She grabbed the taller one with her lips, then reached across the table and offered my mother the other one. There was no smok-ing at Tiny's but after hours, Arlene did it anyway.

"I'm sick of hearing about the fucking earth," she declared, picking up her Zippo lighter, extending the flame across the table to my mother. Then she lit her own cigarette the way she always did—like a Marlboro man, with her head cocked and one eye squinted.

"I couldn't give two shits about this planet," she snickered, a little drunk. My mother laughed. She always took Arlene's side on things.

Even though she and Arlene were friends, my mother never got used to how fond I was of Peter Pam. She was too afraid of losing me. She'd grown up moving in and out with different foster families. In the middle of the night, social services would come and snatch her. So for a long time after I was born she almost never put me down. She told me she even fucked a guy once with me on her hip. "We rode him like a bull!" she'd howled.

With the flick of Arlene's thumb and a tinny *pop,* the flame on her Zippo went out and the lighter closed.

"We'll all be dead soon anyway," Arlene proclaimed.

It was an argument she used for many things and one my mother heartily agreed with.

When Peter Pam finished unloading her bra, she took the mound of trash and deposited it into a paper bag. She rattled the ice in the bottom of her glass and finished her Coke. "I gotta get out of these mules. My feet are killing me." It was one in the morning when she slid out of the booth. She walked through the kitchen out the back to the set of stairs that led to her apartment.

A little while later I got up. I took the last bag of trash out back and was about to hurl it up into the Dumpster when a sound stopped me.

A grunt, a groan. I looked up. There was a car parked at the far end of the parking lot. I heard it again, this time it was louder. I moved closer. When I got within a few feet of the car, I stopped and listened.

The smell of that night's burgers and onion rings hung in the air. A cloud had anchored in the sky and locked in all the heat. A faint sliver of moon lingered at an angle behind it. A bat swooped down overhead and the insects shrieked.

The car was shrouded, but even in the dark the hubcaps gleamed. I held my breath and listened. I heard a low throaty grunt and then a *thud!* After that, a snicker, a sneer. Someone was laughing.

I took a step closer and looked underneath the car. On the far side of it, the streetlamp cast an oval of yellow light. Just under the front tire, lying on its side in the gravel, I saw the mule, extra-large and red. Beyond it were two sets of black boots.

I stood and backed away, quietly. Then turned and ran as fast as I could. Mel hid a key to the gas station on the ledge above the back door. I found an empty paint can in the pile of Peter Pam's junk. I stood on it, felt around, and found the key. I dropped it twice trying to get it in the keyhole. "Come on!" I said. Finally, the key slipped in. I turned the handle and bolted for Mel's office.

He had a gun. Peter Pam had told me Mel kept it in the top drawer of his desk. I yanked it open, and there it was. I ran back out the door and up the parking lot. By the time I got to the car, I was panting. On the far side of it, Peter Pam was pinned facedown to the ground. Half her clothes were ripped off. The guy with the tattoos stood over her. His pants were down. His ass was white, a vein in his erection swelled. The one with the cap stood by snickering.

I caught my breath, readied the gun with both hands, and stepped into the streetlight.

"Let her go, or I'll shoot you dead!" I was trying to channel Clint Eastwood, but my voice shook like Edith Bunker's.

I steadied the gun in my hands. In the corner of my vision, Peter Pam reached out and grabbed her mule. The one with his pants up ran for the woods. But the one I really wanted stood right in front of me.

"Raise your fucking hands or I swear to God I'll pull the trigger." This time I sounded more authentic.

His back was to me and when he put his hands up, the snake on his forearm rippled. I jammed the gun at the center of his bald head. He stiffened.

"Ruthie," Peter Pam said. She was still on the ground a few feet away from me. "Don't shoot." But I wasn't going to listen to her.

My mother was raped once in an alley. I was eleven when it happened. His buddy held me by the neck up against a wall. I had to hear her moan through the hand that covered her mouth and listen to the *huh, huh, huh* of the guy's throaty breath as he pushed himself inside her. They left her on the ground with her skirt pulled up. I was about to run for the police when she stopped me. She looked up at me in the dim dirty light of that night, sighed, and half smiled, like the idea of calling the cops was the sweetest thing she'd ever heard.

This time I knew better. I wasn't going to call anyone, I was just going to shoot him.

I took my thumb and pulled the hammer back slowly.

"Don't do it," Peter Pam said.

I'd never shot a gun, but I had a real good feeling I was going to like it. I looked straight down the barrel. I squeezed the trigger but just as the gun was about to go off, a purse knocked my arm down.

"What the hell are you doing?" my mother said to me. Arlene and my mother must have seen me standing in the streetlight. They were bent over huffing and puffing from running through the parking lot. Before they could see her, Peter Pam snatched her clothes and vanished. My mother finally caught her breath. She looked up and when she noticed the guy standing in front of me with his arms up, and his pants half down, rage lit across her face.

"Give me that thing." She grabbed the gun from me. "I'll fucking shoot him myself." She turned and aimed. "Nobody touches my daughter!"

"Things like this just happen," my mother had explained to me, as if being raped was something she was used to. But this was different. The one thing my mother swore she'd do was kill anyone who laid a hand on me. So that night, when the guy made his move and bolted for the woods, my mother pulled the trigger.

The sound of the gun hit the hot still air. A breeze moved through the branch overhead. A leaf teetered down and landed at my feet. Then everything stopped. There was dead silence.

Gun smoke lingered in the streetlight. My mother and I stood there stunned, waiting to hear a body drop. This was how it would end. It flashed before me: my mother in an orange jumpsuit rotting away in jail. But luckily she had bad aim. My shoulders dropped with relief when I heard the *thump, thump, thump* of his boots pounding hard across the earth.

Arlene had run back to Tiny's and called the cops. They drove up the parking lot at a hundred miles per hour, skidded to a stop, and jumped out. Arlene and my mother worked themselves up talking over each other as they rattled off the details in a frenzy. "He was going to rape my daughter," my mother screamed. "His pants were down!" Arlene added. "I should have killed him," my mother hissed. "I could have done it with my bare hands," Arlene said.

"Ladies, please!" one of the officers yelled before they finally stopped.

A storm was coming. I could smell it in the air. The wind volleyed. The treetops swayed and the silver underside of the leaves turned up. I looked around for Peter Pam but couldn't find her. Then I felt a pair of eyes. Standing in the darkened window of her apartment, she clutched the drape and looked out. Peter Pam was dignified and private. Even from a distance I could feel her sense of shame. When she caught my gaze, she drew the curtain, backed away and disappeared.

They found the guy the next day hiding in the Dumpster behind the high school. We IDed him right away. But I never told what really happened.

CHAPTER SEVENTEEN

Gloom

Peter Pam shut herself up in her apartment claiming she had the flu and I worried she'd never come out. My mother and Arlene hardly noticed, though. They were too busy phoning TV shows.

Arlene thought the story would be perfect for *Good Morning America*, but when she called they put her on hold too long, so she called *The Oprah Winfrey Show* and was now on hold with them. She'd been sitting at our kitchen table drinking coffee and smoking Camels for hours.

"The story is not tragic enough for Oprah," I tried to explain to them. I was on the couch flipping through *People* magazine. "If someone had lost a limb in the incident, it would have been better." Arlene and my mother looked puzzled so I tried to clarify. "And then, if you lost a leg, you'd have to be happy you still had the other one. Oprah once had on this guy who had no arms and no legs. They wheeled him out onto the stage and he told the audience how grateful he was that he could breathe. Oprah clapped and cried and said, 'Wow, now that's gratitude.' She's heavy into gratitude." Bored, I tossed my magazine down on the coffee table. I was sure I'd made perfect sense. But by the looks on their faces I could tell my mother and Arlene didn't think so.

"Fuck Oprah," Arlene abruptly quipped, slamming down the phone. "Let's call *60 Minutes* instead."

Three days passed. Peter Pam still did not come out. She claimed she didn't like people seeing her when she was sick. So we took turns leaving plates of food outside her door.

"Mix in some cream cheese," Arlene instructed. "It's one of her favorites."

Arlene and I were in the kitchen. I was scrambling eggs. She was pouring a cup of coffee.

Then suddenly we heard something: footsteps on the floor above us. I looked at Arlene, she looked at me. She set the coffeepot down. I turned the stove off. We stood still and listened.

There was a clatter. Dave, Peter Pam's cat, knew how to flush the toilet. We heard him overhead meowing and pawing at the handle. For a while there was nothing, but then the door to Peter Pam's apartment squawked the way it always did when it opened. We heard keys rattle, then footsteps descending her staircase.

The back door opened, and—*poof!*—just like that, Peter Pam was gone. A man stood in her place wearing sneakers instead of mules. His jeans were loose fitting and worn. His white shirt was button-down, the sleeves halfway rolled up. His hair was brown, and even though he wasn't yet thirty, it was thinning. His mustache was gone but his beard was at least two days old.

"Well, don't just stand there like a couple of ninnies," he said. "We've got work to do before the morning rush." With Peter

Pam's usual flare, he walked by us, picked up a dish towel, and shooed us along with it. Then he pushed through the kitchen doors.

Peter, the man, swung his hips wide the same way Peter Pam did, and the occasional Yiddish still slipped out, but life without Peter Pam had no humor. Peter didn't talk or laugh much, and every night after work he went straight home.

One night, I was the last one to leave the restaurant. I shut the lights off and pulled the back door closed and when I turned around Peter was sitting on the bottom step gazing at the sky.

I sat down next to him. For a while we looked up and neither one of us spoke.

The sky was deep and clear. Like microscopic ocean life drifting to the bottom, the stars twinkled then receded into dust.

"Compared to the size of the universe, we are only one billionth the size of an ant," he finally said.

We sat there awestruck. A satellite blinked across the sky far, far above us.

"What fools we are to think we matter," he said.

I looked at him. His face was tilted up. The moonlight drew a line down his profile.

"Why were we put here if we don't matter?"

"Apparently God made a mistake," he said.

A breeze crossed our feet. He and I now wore the same shoes—red Converse high-tops. He hugged his knees into his chest. His feet lifted off the ground.

"Atticus Finch would disagree with you." I said. No matter where we started, our conversations always ended up on this, our favorite topic, *To Kill a Mockingbird*. We both believed in aliens and agreed 100 percent, without question, that if they came to Earth and asked for just one book, that's the one we'd give them. It was a triumph how that book showed the human race from so many angles.

Peter Pam would have kept the conversation going, but Peter just sighed. He smiled and tapped me on the knee as if he thought I was being cute.

"It's getting late," he said. "You better go."

So we said good night. He stood up and I got on my bike.

"Ruthie?" he called just before I left.

"Yeah?" I turned and faced him.

The light at the top of the stairs by his apartment door caught his face. His eyes filled with sadness, the kind that settles in and never leaves. A long look passed between us.

"Be careful on that bike," he finally said.

CHAPTER EIGHTEEN

Loss

M y mother bolted upright. "What was that?" She had fallen asleep in her lounge chair.

"McDonald's just got off the power grid," I said.

Every midnight when they closed, their lights went out, and a loud *zap!* left a line of french-fry-smelling smoke drifting in the air.

"Oh, thank God," my mother breathed with a hand across her heart. "It scared me." Relieved, she lay back down. Then she found her half-finished glass of wine on the ground next to her and took a sip.

"What were we talking about again?" she asked. But neither one of us could remember.

We sighed and looked up.

"It's so quiet," she said.

It was creepy how still that summer had become. Some days downtown was so empty you could hear bits of gravel skip along the curb when the breeze kicked up. That night, the day's traffic had muffled to a barely discernible hum. Even Mother Nature was mute—no warbles or peeps or rustling in the leaves.

The one thing we always heard was the Hansons' walking sprinkler. It plodded back and forth across their front lawn at a slow and steady pace throughout the day and night. Hank oiled it every week and Dotty fostered it like a mother; if it ever got stuck, she'd nudge it with her walker and set it moving in the right direction. But one evening the sprinkler strayed and Dotty accidentally ran it over on the street.

They had six similar ones gathering dust on a shelf in their store, but they never replaced it. Within a week their lawn was dead, every green shred of it gone.

In the silence of the night, I thought I heard a noise. I turned around.

"The Hansons' light is on," I said.

"Maybe they're awake."

"They go to bed at eight o'clock."

"Maybe there's something really good on TV."

"They don't have a TV," I said.

My mother fished a gnat out of her wineglass and took another gulp. A tree creaked and a chill tickled the air.

"I'm going to peek in their window," I said.

"You can't do that, she'll think you're a thief and beat you with her walker."

She had a point, so I sat back down. Dotty was a maniac with that walker. Half the town had been bruised by it.

Nick at Night had been running a *Love Boat* marathon all week and when my mother realized we were missing it, we went inside. She had always dreamed of taking a cruise, so this show was one of her favorites. But I couldn't focus.

"What if they're dead?" I said.

"For Chrissake, Ruthie. All right, stay here."

She flung the sheet off and bolted out of bed. The back door slammed shut. I got up and watched her through the window. With her hands tucked under her chin, she tiptoed next door like a rabbit. She stood under the Hansons' window and pricked up an ear to listen, then tiptoed back.

"I hear snoring. Are you happy? My theory," she continued when we got back into bed, "is that they fell asleep with the light on in those two overstuffed chairs they have. And Hank's doesn't have a high back so his head has kind of fallen up against it like this." She propped herself up on her elbows and flung her head back with her eyes closed and her mouth open. Then she flopped back down on the bed. "And the angle of his head and neck has forced his mouth wide open, causing his snoring. That's it. I've figured it out. I'm going to sleep." She reached over the side of the bed, pulled her bag up, and started riffling through it. Apparently it was lipstick time again. When she was done, she chucked it into her purse and let the bag slide to the floor.

I shut the TV off and the blue-green light faded. My mother slipped down under the sheet next to me. A breeze came in through the window and billowed the venetian blind with a soft rattle. The moonlight tumbled over us in stripes. I wrapped my arm around my mother and we spooned together like always.

An hour later, I woke up hearing music. A love song wafted through the air. *My funny valentine, sweet comic valentine. You're my favorite work of art.* Unmistakably Ella Fitzgerald.

At first it was hard to tell where it was coming from. But when I got out of bed and looked next door, I could see them in their window—Dotty and Hank in the middle of their living room, dancing. The warm light above made their faces glow. Holding on to each other, they rocked and moved across the floor like young lovers. It looked easier for them to dance together than it was for either one to walk alone.

When the song was over, their dancing stopped. A moment later, their lights went out.

✧

In her daisy-print dress and wide-brimmed yellow hat, Dotty stepped out first. It was ten the next morning. The two of them shuffled to their car, folded Hank's walker, and placed it in the back. Before Dotty walked around and put her own walker in the car, she straightened out his tie, smoothed a wrinkle on his shoulder, and helped him into the passenger's seat. When she drove off, the purr of their Oldsmobile lingered in the street until they disappeared around the bend.

"You see," my mother said behind me. "They're fine."

✧

The heat in late summer was sharp and searing. The sunlight deadened every color and the lack of rain killed off several trees.

But that afternoon, the sky tore open, the rain poured down in steely sheets, and the wind pummeled the earth in violent gusts.

Two days went by. Our basement flooded. The electricity went out. Fat River swelled and the streets filled with water. Every groove in the earth spilled over. A low desperate groan belched across the town when the roof of the old mill building crumbled.

On the third day, the downpours stopped. The sky slowly brightened. A meager rainbow tried to arch across the street, but a dagger of sunlight sizzled up its spine and—*zap!*—just like that, it was gone.

We opened our door and looked out. The thrum of water was everywhere. It trickled down gutters, swirled down pipes, and dripped off branches. A river gushed along the street. Shiny bits of garbage caught the light and glinted in the water. Bigger things bobbed about. I counted two umbrellas, a cordless phone, two baseball caps. A flip-flop and a pair of mangled glasses had landed on our front steps. Someone's lawn chair was angled in the bush in front of Patti's.

Patti opened her front door and waved across the rushing water. Looking out her picture window, Miss Frankfurt cradled Pancake to her cheek. But next door, the Hansons' house was quiet. Their shades were drawn. No sign of life was seen or heard so we sloshed across the way. When we rang the doorbell, the only sound it mustered was a soggy burp, so we knocked. And knocked again until we were pounding and screaming at the door.

There was a clatter across the street. In his bright orange chest-high waders, Roger stepped out of his door with his chainsaw, another Walmart purchase, in one hand. He raised the other to shield his eyes and took a moment to look around.

Patti pointed him in our direction and, as if he wore a cape, he plunged down off their steps and waded through the street.

"Stand back!" he shouted when he got to us. "I've been dying to use this." And he fired up the engine. With four gritty throttles, he cut a square hole through their door and stepped through. We waited on the Hansons' dead and flooded lawn.

"Every kid should have a bike," Hank had said that summer

when he had mine upside down in the back of his store. By that time, my bike had become more like a Batmobile. Dotty insisted that Hank give me new brakes, side mirrors, a headlight, and a taillight that blinked when I turned. Every Saturday he greased my gears so that when I pedaled uphill it was easy. And he made sure my tires were always pumped just right so that if I ever hit a bump, I wouldn't feel it.

The only time Hank talked was when his hands were busy. It was as if the act of moving them unlocked a secret door. He quoted poetry from people I'd never heard of, and he knew every phrase that Jesus ever uttered. And every time he started talking, without fail, Dotty would shuffle down the aisle. "Don't be yakking her ear off, Hank! For Chrissake, she's probably hungry!" And she'd raise and rattle a Tupperware container full of cookies she'd baked the night before.

Their grand reopening had generated only a temporary bump in sales. For a while they ran a TV ad, and in July they'd hired a mascot. A guy dressed up as a hammer stood out in front of the store and waved the American flag. But three more departments at the plastic tubing company had moved to China and business everywhere had slowed. And they were tired, I could tell. Every time I saw them, they seemed a little weaker.

When Roger appeared again in the opening of the door, his face was white.

"God's grace," Hank said to me that last time I saw him, "is in the wind that whips around you when you're coasting. Every kid deserves to have that feeling."

I later learned that the day I saw them leave their house, they'd gone to church, after years of not going, and renewed their wedding vows. When they came home they shared an apple and lay down together fully clothed, as if to take a nap.

Peppered with dead flies, the apple core was on the floor beside their bed. They had peeled it and soaked it overnight in poison.

CHAPTER NINETEEN

Redemption

The flood left an ashen pallor. The stench of waste ripened in the sun. A lump settled in my throat. Life seemed to be falling apart. Fewer people were eating out and my mother's tips began to dwindle.

But for a while, after the Hansons died, a wistfulness enshrouded the town. Hushed tones and sweet words laced every conversation. Arlene took her husband back even though she'd kicked him out again just two weeks before. My mother and I hugged every time we parted and people who hadn't been to Tiny's in months came back to share a meal.

Then one day, on my mother's day off, a 1970 Lincoln Continental pulled into the parking lot. When the restaurant door swung open and Miss Frankfurt stepped inside, mouths dropped. Forks hit plates, coffee mugs lowered. The handful of customers, all of them former students, looked at her and held their breath as if anticipating a scolding.

Miss Frankfurt had not been to Tiny's in over fifteen years.

But here she was standing in the doorway clutching a quilted hen-shaped purse. Her swollen ankles bulged around her shoes. She wore a gray skirt suit with a mauve scarf, just a touch of sensible color. Her hair was twirled into a neat bun and her glasses were the same vintage as her car. They had upside-down arms and the lenses were huge. Her mouth turned down and bracketed the ball of her chin. Her lower lip protruded. She sucked it in and out as she looked around for a seat.

When I saw her across the street working in her garden, she seemed soft and kind, but up close, she terrified me. In class I'd look around and there she'd be standing in the back like a ghost. Her arms crossed at her ample bosom, she'd watch the teacher's every move.

She scooted into the nearest booth, dragging her purse along the table. When she was squarely in the center, she let her heft drop. Pushing up on her hair, she gathered herself from the effort. She unzipped the hen purse and pulled out a smaller identical change purse and set it on the table. Then she settled the larger hen on the seat next to her.

Peter Pam's real name was Peter Montgomery. Of all Miss Frankfurt's former students, Peter had been her most promising. She had no children of her own and she'd pinned her hopes on him, certain he'd be the one to leave this town and make her proud.

But he never moved away or went to college. Peter Montgomery was a natural-born ham. There wasn't a single thing not to like about him and nobody cared that he wore a dress. But Miss Frankfurt was Catholic. She called it sinful, witless, and foolish and swore she'd never speak to him again.

He stood in front of the counter trembling. His mouth hung open, a half-empty coffeepot shaking in his hand.

Miss Frankfurt pulled her glasses down her nose and searched the room. When she saw him, her eyes stopped. A moment passed between them.

"Well," she finally said, "don't just stand there like a dimwit. For God's sake, pour me a cup of coffee."

Peter managed to pour her coffee without spilling it and bring her an English muffin without dropping it. Then he burst through the kitchen doors and nearly fainted. "I can't breathe!" he choked, doubling over. He reached for the upside-down plastic bucket inside the door. Arlene grabbed his arm and eased him down onto it before he fell. She fanned him for a while with a menu.

And I stood watch. Through the round window in the kitchen door I saw Miss Frankfurt drink her coffee. She spread orange marmalade on her muffin so intently she didn't seem to notice that everyone was watching her.

"She's done," I reported when she'd finished her last bite.

"Oh, God," Peter moaned.

"Okay, that's enough of this, I've had it," Arlene said, chucking the menu down on the counter. "Get up," she chided, "and quit being a baby." She grabbed Peter's elbow and pulled him up.

She placed her hands on his shoulders and looked him in the eye. "Listen up," she said as if she were his coach. "You are a beautiful person, do you hear me?" Arlene grazed her hand over his forehead. "And God made you, same as her. Now I want you to go out there and stand tall. I want you to look down that big beautiful nose of yours and hand her the check as if she was a speck of dust to you."

"Okay, okay," Peter said apprehensively. "I think I can do it."

"Of course you can." Arlene clocked him on the shoulder, annoyed.

"Ruthie," she snapped. Without taking her eyes off Peter she reached behind her where I stood ready with the check. She took it and placed it in Peter's hand.

"Now go!" Arlene said, shoving him out the door.

Arlene and I each took a window. Peter hadn't moved. He stood frozen just outside the door. Arlene shouldered it into him, nudging him forward. He finally started, but just before he reached her table, his knees buckled and he had to steady himself on the edge of it.

"Oh, God," Arlene grumbled.

Peter went to hand Miss Frankfurt the check but his arm shook and the check trembled. Aggravated, Miss Frankfurt reached up and snatched it right out of the air.

A moment passed.

Peter quaked.

You could hear a pin drop. Arlene and I stepped out through the kitchen door. I looked around. The customers had all stopped midaction. They held their breath, waiting to hear Miss Frankfurt explode. But nothing happened. She opened her change purse and handed Peter a bill. He cowered, hesitating.

"For God's sake, take the money," Miss Frankfurt snapped, and waved it in his face.

He inched the bill from her hand, careful not to upset her more, then slowly turned to go.

Miss Frankfurt scooted out to the edge of the booth, dropped her head, and lifted herself up with effort.

"Mr. Montgomery," she called when she saw him tiptoeing away from her.

His shoulders dropped, resigned.

"Look at me when I speak to you."

He sheepishly turned around.

The waning afternoon sun streamed in through the windows. Miss Frankfurt lowered her glasses. The creases on her upper lip deepened as she pinched her mouth. Her gaze bore down on him and the unadorned silver crucifix around her neck caught the light. A long tense moment passed.

"I have prayed on it now for many years. The other day, the good Lord finally spoke. 'Frankfurt,' he said to me, 'stop fussing over foolishness. It's not what you wear or who you are with, it's what's in your soul that matters.'"

Peter stood in disbelief. He turned on his heels and looked at us. Wide-eyed, he clutched himself as if to say, *Did you just hear that?* He turned back to her. I could feel his heart swell. He was just about to throw his arms around her when she held a hand up to stop him.

"Let's not get carried away now," she said.

"No, no, of course not," Peter said, retreating quickly.

She walked by him, put her hand on the door to push it open, but then stopped. She turned around again.

"I will agree with you on one thing, though." She looked him up and down. "You look much better in a dress." Something at his neck caught her gaze. Her expression hardened. "And fix your collar, would you?" She made a gesture at her neck. "It's all folded in." I hadn't noticed, but it was.

When Miss Frankfurt drove out of the parking lot, an empty Walmart bag spun in her wake. Her tires left a streak of dust, and—*poof!*—just like that, she set the world straight again. Three days later a new pair of mules arrived and Peter Pam was back.

CHAPTER TWENTY

Jealousy

A nimals are smarter than we are," Peter Pam declared. "They can predict all kinds of natural disasters. Cows will lie down before it rains and cats and dogs are more likely to run away before an earthquake."

She and I were sitting in the back booth talking up a storm. Unlike Arlene, Peter Pam couldn't do a single trick. She couldn't even whistle. "My lips just don't purse up right," she'd explained, puckering them to show me. But I had missed her terribly. It was fall again and I was back in school. I would ride my bike to Tiny's every afternoon just to be with her.

Our chatter, I could tell, was infuriating my mother. I could see her in the corner of my eye wiping and rewiping the tables around us with an irritated edge. It was Arlene's day off so there was no one to distract her.

"And a tsunami will drown us all, but the animals will run for the hills. The entire kingdom will empty out."

I looked out the window searching for the family of squirrels that lived in the tree across the street, but didn't see a single one.

Tiny's had been quiet for months. Mel took a pay cut so no one else had to, but our bills were piling up. My mother was beginning to lose all her graceful movements. Things she used to savor, like the smell of McDonald's, bothered her. Half the time our chairs out back were an eyesore, a reminder that we didn't have a pool. And Arlene was getting on her nerves.

My mother pushed the chairs in with loud, angry scrapes, but Peter Pam had too much pent-up energy to notice.

"A dog can predict a seizure up to three hours before it happens. Oh my goodness," Peter Pam said, taking a breath. "I'm all farklemt." She fluttered her hands in front of her face in an effort to tamp her emotions. "It's so good to talk to you again." She reached across the table and held my arm.

My mother's lip curled and I wanted to disappear. My relationship with Peter Pam grated on her. She was about to snap, I could tell, but thankfully, a customer pulled into the parking lot. Customers were rare these days, so it was enough to stop her. And this customer drove a brand-new BMW.

The driver's-side door opened slowly and, of all people, Vick Ward stepped out.

"Gross," I said to my mother. But she was not listening. She chucked her rag down. She ruffled her hair and set it cascading down her face in perfect peekaboo fashion. Then she unbuttoned her top button, shook her breasts down into her bra, and pushed them up again.

When she really wanted something she showed them off like cakes. "You've got to think of them as assets. They can be leverage or incentive or payback," she'd instructed, as if she were a banker. She'd been taking chicken wings out of the microwave when she told me this. She held up her lobster-claw oven mitt, pinched it together, and said, "They can be handy like pot holders!"

In the parking lot, Vick Ward straightened his tie and then looked down at his shoes. He took a handkerchief out of his breast pocket, bent over, and with two quick flicks of his wrist dusted the toes. Then he shook the cloth out, folded it up, and replaced it in his pocket.

He walked in, stood in the doorway, and looked around. When he saw my mother, he tipped his hat in her direction, then slid into the nearest booth.

My mother was sassy and rude to him like she'd been the day he first came to our house, but things had changed since then. We were broke again, so she did what she thought she had to. She reached over him extra close and flirted while she served him. And it paid off like it always did.

He left my mother a ten-dollar tip on pie and coffee—the only decent tip she got all week.

CHAPTER TWENTY-ONE

Betrayal

Across the street, Roger lost his job and Patti found part-time work at Walmart. She stopped coming by and they stopped eating at Tiny's. We never thought we would, but we missed them.

In October, the trucks were back, but instead of bringing stuff in, Patti and Roger were selling things and moving it out. This sent my mother further into panic. And when she panicked, it frightened me. She became quiet and removed. Her jaw muscles tightened. I could never tell what she was thinking and I was too afraid to ask.

One night that fall, she was really late getting home from work and I began to worry. So I hopped on my bike and rode to Tiny's.

I pulled into the parking lot and around back. *Pop!* The gravel crunched beneath my tires. I heard Madonna—*"Holiday! Celebrate!"*—my mother's favorite, playing on the stereo as I headed toward the kitchen. The screen door was propped open with a can of tomato sauce.

I stepped in. The overhead light above the grill was on. The mop sat in the sink in a pool of dirty water. I ducked under the handle and walked by. There was an empty bottle of wine and a couple of glasses sitting on the counter. One of the glasses had toppled over and landed against a plate with a lipstick-stained napkin and a few leftover fries. The plate next to it was licked clean. I walked through the kitchen and stood behind the counter. The restaurant was dark but the neon hot dog still flashed in and out of its bun. Then I heard something. A cough. A gag. And it wasn't coming from Madonna. The sound was coming from the bathrooms, so I stepped out from behind the counter and followed it. A slick of light seeped out from under the door of the ladies' room. I pushed it open and walked in. Madonna's voice followed me. *"Oh yeah, oh yeah,"* she grunted through the speakers on the wall.

I heard a heavy sigh then a low whispery moan from inside one of the stalls. I slowly pushed the first door open, but it was empty. The handicapped stall was already halfway open so I took a step forward and peered in.

I could recognize my mother from a million miles away—by the way she swung her arms when she walked or the way she crossed and hugged them to her body when she was cold. I could hear the subtle shift in the tone of her voice before and then after she'd had her coffee. I knew almost everything about her.

But that night, I didn't recognize her until I saw her purse. She was kneeling on it. She was facing the toilet and her head was bobbing up and down, to the rhythm of Madonna.

He was easier to identify—with his hat on backwards, Mel straddled the toilet. His pants were down. His eyes were closed.

His lids were white. His mouth was half open. He gripped the grab bar on the wall. A bead of sweat rolled down his neck.

He must have sensed me standing there because his eyes flew open.

"Jesus!" he yelled over Madonna when he saw me.

My mother lifted her head and turned. Her lipstick was smeared—her mouth glistened bloodred like she'd been eating prey.

A single overhead light flickered. A second passed—not even—and I was out the door, flying through the night. I landed on my bike with my legs already in motion. I pedaled so fast, the sweat on my forehead dried in seconds. A truck pulled up behind me. I stood in my seat and pumped harder. A piece of gravel shot up and ricocheted off the frame of my glasses. But I didn't flinch. I turned my wheels and took the shortcut—a path that led into the woods—just dodging the cloud of dust the truck stirred up in its wake.

The woods were dark and the crickets were throwing a tantrum. I slowed down, tried to catch my breath, but my heart pounded and swelled as if it might burst right through my chest.

The moonlight fell between the leaves in patches and flickered like scratchy film. The ground beneath me shifted. I stopped, got off my bike, and braced myself against a tree.

Every man I ever knew had something dark and horrible hidden inside of him, but Mel was different. He didn't drink. He didn't swear, he never yelled. And he was unlike any man I knew: he never leered at my mother and he was faithful to his wife, even though she really was the Ice Queen. But my mother ruined men.

An owl lifted off the branch above me. A swirl of leaves fell. It felt as though the sky was falling. It had been a fluke that time had passed and nothing bad had happened. Now, it seemed, our luck was running out. Mother Earth was gearing up to shrug us off like flies.

✧

When I got home, my mother was already there. She said something but I walked right past her, microwaved some popcorn, and left her sipping through a straw on her giant cup of rum and Diet Coke. She was drunk and getting drunker.

I kicked my sneakers off so they hit the wall on purpose. I got into bed and flipped through the channels, desperate to lose myself in some overwrought melodrama. Thank God they play reruns of *ER* all the time.

On *ER* there are no regular accidents. There are tornados and plane crashes. Olympic swimmers lose their legs, fourth-degree burns turn movie stars into monsters. The hospital itself catches fire on a regular basis. I found an episode and was hooked right away.

"Aren't you going to say anything?" my mother asked. I hadn't noticed, but she'd followed me and was now standing in the bedroom doorway. I shoveled popcorn into my mouth and ignored her. She shook her ice and took a purposefully loud slurp from the bottom of her cup. Then, in and out, in and out, she pumped the straw through the top so it squeaked. It was so annoying.

On-screen, an explosion outside the hospital shook the IV bags. The lights flicked on and off and the building filled with smoke. One after another, the nurses and EMTs wheeled patients in. And in between all the chaos and coughing the doctors barked a stream of indecipherable orders.

"Don't play this game with me," my mother sneered.

Half the city was now burning and the place was jammed. The camera shook. Sirens wailed. A woman was convulsing, then the beeping of her heart flattened out. "Clear!" The doctor shouted.

"It's not like I fucked him," my mother slurred.

In rapid building sequence, from one disaster to another, images flashed back and forth.

"Don't be such a goddamn prude." My mother turned to go.

"Trash," I muttered as she headed through the door.

My mother grabbed the doorframe to stop herself from falling forward. She teetered, took a huge breath, swung her head low, and turned around. With her eyes ablaze, she flared her nostrils, raised her head, and the alcohol on her breath ignited. "You think you're so high and mighty, don't you? Well, let me tell you something. If I lost my job right now we'd die on the streets."

We had always heard home ownership was a pathway out of poverty but it was leading us down a hole to hell. Our monthly mortgage bill had gone up so fast, it had almost doubled. We'd missed one payment already. We'd fallen further behind on all our other bills and my mother had stopped sleeping.

She stepped closer, shook a crooked finger at me, and I turned the volume up.

"You should be thanking me. You think Mel's above it all, don't you? Well, let me tell you, when push comes to shove, he's just like every boss, all he cares about is money. He'd lay me off in a heartbeat if I didn't give him reason not to."

George Clooney's surgical mask pulsated in and out and

he dripped with sweat. He was cutting through bone when—*splat!*—a piece of bloody flesh flew up and hit him in the goggles.

"Not a single one of them could give two shits about us. You're a fool if you think they do. When it comes right down to it, I'm the one who takes you with me when I go!"

My mother spun around and lurched to leave the room, but missed the door and hit the frame instead. She staggered, and then—*bam!*—flat on her back she hit the floor.

I looked down at her, registered that she was still breathing, then turned the volume up. I crammed another fistful of popcorn into my mouth.

"Weight gain, insomnia, heart palpitations, diarrhea, and in rare cases death or stroke." An antidepressant commercial was on and the list of potential side effects made depression itself sound fun.

My mother coughed. Then she gagged. I glanced at her again. A bubble of vomit parted her lips. I sighed, rolled my eyes, tossed my bowl of popcorn aside, got up off the bed, and turned her over. "Not on your back," I said.

A bruised and bloody woman swaddling a dead baby crashed through the emergency-room doors. A doctor in another room cut a tumor out. He placed the glistening bloody mass neatly on a stainless-steel tray, then a nurse whisked it out as if to serve it hot.

I grabbed my mother by the hips and held her up. "Come on, Mom," I pleaded, and gave her a little shake. "Spit it up."

In my dream that night, Anne Frank, Mother Mary, and Hillary Clinton were all sitting at a table. Like writers on a TV show, they were brainstorming my ending.

"She's enslaved in a dungeon. She is starved and beaten. But when she dies, her suffering makes her a hero," Anne Frank said.

"Don't be stupid," Mother Mary retorted. "She's worshiped in perpetuity for her submissiveness before man and God."

Hillary Clinton let out a snort. "Let's be real. This girl's story is going to end exactly how it began. In a run-down, rat-infested hovel with her crazy mother. Now snap out of your stupor. Let's work together and get something done."

CHAPTER TWENTY-TWO

Forgiveness

R uthie! Ruthie!" My eyes slowly focused. "Wake up." My mother stood over me holding my clothes. "We overslept, you'll be late for school."

I hardly ever missed a day of school. She kept two alarm clocks by her head and if we slept through them, she'd drive a hundred miles an hour the wrong direction on a one-way street just to get me there. It was the only reason she ever left the house without makeup, and no hangover ever stopped her.

She took my arm, guided me out of bed, and pulled me into the kitchen. She still reeked of alcohol. "You can change in the car. Here," she said, and grabbed a box off the table. "Have a Pop-Tart." She thrust them at me and, like that, we were out the door.

I put my jeans on, slipped into my long-sleeved T-shirt, and rode in silence.

"You've got two minutes," she said, looking at the dashboard clock, skidding to a stop in front of school. "Now go!"

A mass of hair was heaped on top of her head. Her roots were showing and her hair clip was falling out. Her skin looked almost gray. She'd lost weight and the pockets underneath her eyes were swollen. The one nearest to me twitched.

I was still half asleep so she reached across, opened my door, and pushed me out. Bleary-eyed, I made it halfway up the steps to the door when my mother shouted, "Wait!" I turned around. Still in her slippers and robe, she was running toward me.

"Your paper," she panted, and handed it to me. "They're really going to want to read this one. It's brilliant."

I made a face. My mother claimed that about all my papers.

"I mean it," she said. "I think it may be your best one yet." Even though I knew she didn't understand half of them, she kept all my papers neatly preserved in a three-ring binder.

"Now go. And you better run."

"From Slavery to the Holocaust and Beyond: An Examination of the Decline of the Human Race." She handed me my paper and I took off. Just before I pulled the school doors open, I looked back and saw her. She was sitting up in the seat, looking at herself in the mirror, a tube of lipstick in her hand.

She would only wonder why her knees hurt and she'd marvel at the bump on her head. And I would only swallow. And swallow again until the lump inside my throat subsided.

I was walking home from school that day when it began to pour. The clouds were low and heavy. The sky was dark. I put my head down, adjusted my baseball cap, and soldiered on.

I had less than a mile to go when I heard the slither of tires on wet pavement come up behind me. On the one-way street, the car pulled up and slowed.

"Want a ride?" the driver asked, rolling down the window.

I looked up and realized it was Mel.

"Nope," I said, picking up my pace to get away from him.

He stepped on the gas lightly and caught up with me.

"Okay," he shouted over the rain, "how about an umbrella?"

Then he drove his truck halfway up the curb. He reached his body out the window, stuck his arm out, and opened up an oversized umbrella.

"Pfft," I said, throwing my head back, not stopping. The wind had picked up and was blowing the rain sideways so the umbrella was useless anyway.

"I'll drive the whole way like this if I have to." He was steering with one hand and holding the umbrella with the other. "It would be much easier if you just got in."

I stopped short on the sidewalk, crossed my arms, and shot him a dirty look.

"Please, Ruthie, just let me give you a ride home." I looked up at him. His face was red and he was sweating. The rain fell off the edge of his cap in strings like tinsel. His glasses were slipping off his nose. He tilted his head back and tried to look through them anyway. "Please," he said again.

I kicked the mud on the side of the road and it hit the door of his truck. A little clump of it sailed up and landed on his arm.

"Don't expect me to talk to you," I snarled.

I stomped around, climbed in, and slammed the door shut.

Mel closed the umbrella, gave it a shake out the window, and pulled it back in. He leaned it on the seat between us and settled himself behind the wheel.

"Phew." He lifted off his hat and wiped the sweat off his brow with his forearm. He took his glasses off, opened his mouth wide like he was about to swallow the lenses, and—*ha, ha*—breathed one quick hot breath onto each one. Then he tugged on his shirttail and wiped them off.

"Are we just going to sit here? Or are you going to take me home?" I asked.

"Oh, right." He put his glasses back on, pulled the shift stick on the steering wheel toward him and drove off.

I looked out the window and flattened myself against the door, trying to stay as far away from him as possible. A Styrofoam coffee cup rolled around at my feet. His truck smelled like sticky buns and gasoline. The rain kept coming, banging on the roof. The wipers were on high, flapping and squeaking and smacking but never keeping up with it. Mel inched along—like a total sissy, if you asked me.

"Jeez," he said, "I gotta pull over." I rolled my eyes. He glided slowly to a stop, put the car in park, and turned his hazards on.

A giant crack of thunder boomed and a gust of wind shook the truck. I gripped my seat but before I knew it, the wind had set us down again.

"My God, would you look at that?" Mel said.

I turned and looked. He was sitting forward, staring out the window. As if pulled by a string, a train of clouds glided into place in front of us. They split the sky and shot the earth with bolts of lightning. Veins and capillaries of light ran ragged everywhere. A row of pine trees swayed. With another clap of thunder, a wall of rain came at us. Then, abruptly, all went still. The trees stopped rocking. The sky gathered up the lightning and the caravan of clouds moved on.

Flap-flap-squeak. Flap-flap-squeak. Neither of us talked but the windshield wipers kept going. The downpour had turned to drizzle. I figured I could finish walking home now, but just before I pulled the door open, he spoke.

"Svetlana hates me with good reason." When Mel wasn't explaining how something worked, he rarely talked. When he did, he used short, unadorned sentences. His words came out slowly but they always left the impression there was a deeper meaning hidden behind them. And he never talked about Svetlana, so I couldn't help but stop and listen.

"It was raining that night, too." His voice was strange and distant. "There was a thick fog everywhere. I was young and drunk and I was driving the car. I shouldn't have been and Svetlana tried to stop me. 'Pull the damn car over!' she kept screaming."

I turned and looked at him. He was staring straight ahead in a trance. "But I wouldn't stop, so when we got to a light at the top of the bridge she jumped out, ran around, opened my door, and tried pulling me out. She yanked at my arm over and over again. But you know, I'm bigger than she is and the rain was coming down in buckets and we were soaking wet. She grabbed me with both hands, pulled back with all her weight, and gave me one last tug. But then her hands slipped, and she went whirling. She tried to catch her balance, but she stumbled backwards into the fog until she was in the middle of the street."

"It only took an instant." Mel paused for a moment. "I watched it all happen. The light turned green and a Wise potato-chip truck barreled through the mist and hit her. I remember everything. She was wearing a dress. It was silk and printed with red poppies. When I think about it now, it seems beautiful. Her dress fluttered as she tumbled up the windshield and somersaulted over the roof. I half expected her to stick the landing—arch her back, throw her arms up, and face her audience smiling, like I'd seen her do so many times before. But she didn't. She landed in front of me with a thud. The truck slammed on its brakes and just before it careened off the bridge, the back door flew open. Hundreds of single-serve bags spilled out of their boxes and buried her. Splashes of red from her dress winked in between the shimmering blue foil. Her face glowed, her eyes blinked. She looked every bit as breathtaking nestled in those chips as Bette Midler in her bed of roses."

There was a catch in his throat and his voice trailed off. He was still looking off into the distance. Mini-wipers reflected in his glasses. *Flap-flap-squeak, flap-flap-squeak.*

"Why are you telling me this?" I asked.

"Because if we could have had a kid, I'd want a kid just like you, full of wit and smarts. And because I've never told anyone the truth before. And if there is anyone who deserves to know the truth, it's you. The truth is, I am deeply flawed. And the only chance I have at your forgiveness is owning up to it."

The vinyl squeaked as he twisted in his seat to look at me. He swallowed hard.

My chin quivered. I bit my bottom lip to keep from crying.

"Of everyone I know," he said, "you deserve better."

No one had ever said those words to me before. I wanted more than anything to believe him.

CHAPTER TWENTY-THREE

Illness

In early November 2007, the chairs out back filled with mummies of snow. The windows at Hanson's Hardware were boarded up. Overnight they were covered with graffiti. Trucks finally came and emptied out their house, leaving the neighborhood with a gaping hole. Across the street, Patti and Roger had a week-long yard sale. What they couldn't sell, they dragged out to the street with a sign that read, FOR FREE. The stress of everything made my mother sick. She got a cold that lingered for weeks, then the cold became a cough and the cough got so bad she tore a muscle in her neck and broke three ribs. She had sweats and chills. I missed over a week of school staying home to cool her down and warm her up.

She had been sick like this once, years ago, and ended up in the emergency room. We waited hours for the doctor to tell us she had pneumonia and send us home with pills. We *never*—not now or ever—had health insurance. Even though the visit took fifteen minutes at most, we got stuck with this enormous bill.

And the bill kept coming. Everywhere we moved in California it followed us. A debt collector tracked us down and scared us half to death pounding on our apartment door.

So this time when I told her she had to go to the hospital, she harnessed just enough strength to sit up in bed, look at me soberly, and say, "Over my dead body am I going there."

The days dragged on. Mel sent over a glazed ham. Arlene dropped off soup. Peter Pam kept me company every chance she could.

On day six, Miss Frankfurt left lasagna at our door. On the evening of day eight she left a note.

Dear Ruthie,

I have had my uncle contact my cousin—his son—in Boston. My cousin made a few phone calls and I've arranged to have a doctor from Albany come see your mother tomorrow free of charge. She will be arriving at 10 A.M.

Your neighbor,
Mary Elizabeth Frankfurt

I was dumbfounded. I had only ever known her as Miss Frankfurt, the principal of my high school. She was tough and grim and everybody was afraid of her.

I looked across the street, but except for a dim light in her den, the house was dark. Patti had told us she sat there in the evenings reading and I imagined her in her favorite chair, a floor lamp at her side, lost in something good like *I Know Why the Caged Bird Sings* by Maya Angelou.

✧

The doctor arrived right on time. She gave my mother antibiotics, prescription cough medicine, and anti-inflammatory pain relievers. She looked down my mother's throat and taped her ribs. She even called and checked on us the next morning. My mother slowly got better. Two days later, she got out of bed and on the day after that, I went back to school.

The next time I saw Miss Frankfurt it was in between classes. She stood outside her office with her arms crossed, overseeing the hallway, inspecting her students as they passed. I caught her eye to acknowledge what she had done for us. But Miss Frankfurt was the kind of person who had no interest in sentimental thank-yous. She glanced at me stoically, nodded once, then looked away.

CHAPTER TWENTY-FOUR

Extinction

One morning right after that I woke up and found my mother staring out the window.

"They're gone," she mumbled.

As if the bank had repossessed their souls, in the middle of the night Patti and Roger had vanished. All that remained was a tipped-over Big Wheel and the protest of their screen door banging against their empty house in the breeze.

My mother sighed and her breath left a fog on the window. She stood there a while and when she turned and looked at me, dread sickened her eyes.

When you live so close to it, the bottom is never far away. And it is so far from the top that from there we probably look like ants spoiling a picnic. We could all die and nobody would miss us.

"It'll be okay," I said, even though I felt like crying.

She looked at me and shook her head. We were next and she and I both knew it.

My mother had lost almost two weeks of work when she was

sick and we'd fallen further behind on our bills. We'd missed two more mortgage payments and our first foreclosure letter had arrived just the other day. And business at Tiny's had slowed so much, it was impossible to see how we'd ever catch up.

My mother swallowed hard. I could see the lump of fear rising in her throat. Her knees buckled. She collapsed into the kitchen chair and grabbed her pack of cigarettes. She fumbled it, so I took the pack and pulled one out for her. Her hands quaked so I held it to her mouth. She pinched it in her lips and I lit it with a match.

She was crumbling right in front of me. I could almost see her breaking apart into tiny little pieces, leaving nothing but a pile of ash.

Late one night I was lying in bed watching *Seinfeld* when she stumbled in the door drunk. I heard her bag hit the table. She tripped over something on the floor. I waited for the sound of her falling. When I heard her huffing and puffing, I got up and peered down the hallway. She was madly tearing the cushions off the couch, looking for something. When she finished, she staggered over to the kitchen table and started pawing through a pile of junk. She sighed, exhausted, looked up then down the hallway. Before she saw me, I ducked and dove back into bed. When she was like this, just the sight of me could set her off.

A few minutes later I heard the trash cans outside clatter. I got up again and looked out the side window.

Coffee grounds, Big Mac wrappers, scraps of old food, empty

cigarette packs, used tampons—my mother was digging through the trash. A cigarette drooped from the corner of her mouth.

It was cold out. The glow from the window outlined her in a parallelogram of light. Snowflakes appeared as they passed through the darkness. A fragment of the moon dangled above her as if by a breakable thread.

She looked small and frail. A deep line bisected her brow as she sifted through a stack of scratch tickets. She picked up each one and double-checked the numbers. Her nail polish was chipped, her fingers chapped and red, one of her knuckles split and bleeding.

An ash fell. A ticket caught on fire. She shook it, *ouch!* The embers floated up when she tossed it up behind her. And my mother just kept digging, leaning deeper and deeper into the garbage.

When she came in, I heard her vomit. She took a shower. She brushed her teeth. When she got into bed and fell asleep I went outside, picked up the garbage, and secured the lids.

That night I dreamed of floods. The last of the polar ice caps collapsed into the sea. Snatching chunks of land and pulling them under, the ocean engulfed the earth. I escaped on the tail of Florida, but then a tidal wave obliterated me.

I woke with a start. It was still dark outside. In the cold hours before dawn, a gust of wind barreled down our street. It tipped over our garbage with alarming ease. It smacked at the earth and our trash erupted into a twister. The oak tree out front shuddered. With a belch, it heaved. The root system upended and the tree keeled over. It fell away from the house and sprayed the window with dirt.

This could be how it ends. The credits would roll over time-lapse footage of the decomposing tree. There would be no theme or overarching meaning to our story. Just a drawn-out anonymous dying. The kind of dying people like us tend to do.

But dawn came like it always did: with the crow cawing on the telephone wire outside the bedroom window. A brand-new thread of sunlight frayed the horizon line behind it.

At noon my mother got up with a restful glow. She shuffled into the kitchen and poured herself a cup of coffee.

"Look what happened," I said, pointing at the tree lying on the ground.

There is a tipping point, Peter Pam had told me, when the earth will become so hot, the leaves on the trees will curl up and catch fire like they do when you angle a magnifying glass at them.

My mother gazed groggily at the fallen tree. She yawned and scratched her head. "Oh well," she sighed, and shuffled back to bed.

CHAPTER TWENTY-FIVE

Fear

*T*he human race is a godless self-destructive one. It destroys its habitation and eats its own. This was now the universal theme to all of my school papers.

My current paper tackled Darwinism: "We are evolving backwards. Our brains are getting bigger but malfunctioning more." I was sitting at our kitchen table rounding out my argument in my usual way—with one or two indecipherable sentences (it was amazing what an impression this made!)—when my mother emerged from the bathroom.

She came careening toward me down the hall with her arms raised and her head stuck in the neck of a brand-new dress. When she emerged from it, her hair was a different color. She was now a dark brunette.

"Will you zip me up?" she asked, spinning around in front of me. She held her hair off her neck and waited.

Something had changed. She was perky and she smelled of high-priced perfume.

"Hurry." She stepped closer and lowered her back. "Or I'll be late."

"Where are you going?" I asked, zipping her up. But she didn't answer. She dropped her hair, grabbed her coat and bag. "Don't wait up for me," she said, and was out the door.

I looked outside expecting to see her get in the car and drive off, but she didn't. She stood on the side of the road as if she were waiting for a bus. She rubbed her hands together and exhaled into the hollows of her cupped palms. Steam rose from her breath. A car pulled up and my mother got in.

Mice were living in our walls. I had visions of being overrun. At night they lurked in every darkened corner. By day they were brazen and bold. I saw one once angling a Dorito across the floor like a carpenter with a sheet of plywood.

Peter Pam brought me mousetraps. They were extra-roomy "condos." "When you catch them," she'd explained, "you walk them out and open both doors."

But my mother had thrown the condos away and sprinkled the house with poison. Every living critter was now dying: the insects in handfuls like raisins behind the toilet, the mice in corners in pairs on their backs, as if they had been in the middle of a synchronized-swimming routine when they expired.

The leak in our ceiling had gotten worse and we couldn't afford to fix it. Our toilet was broken and overflowed almost daily. Life stunk of death and shit and poison. But my mother didn't notice. She had found what she was looking for when she was digging through the garbage: Vick Ward's home phone number, written on a napkin. She was now out with him all the time.

✧

That next Saturday between lunch and breakfast at Tiny's, I was sweeping the floor when he pulled up. He slithered in so quietly, I didn't see him until he was standing just inside the door.

The suit he wore was precisely tailored with crisp lines and sharp planes of blue fabric. His hair was dyed an unnatural pitch-black, and, like Regis Philbin, he plucked his eyebrows.

With a toothpick in his mouth, he sized up the place. When he saw me, his lips widened into a grin.

"Hey, how you doing, kid?" Vick was overly friendly and had a booming voice. He could spot the only other customer across the aisle or two rows down and start a conversation: "Hey there." He'd stick his head out of his booth. "What are you having?" And he'd keep talking to them even when they'd turned away.

In his shiny leather shoes, Vick walked past me and ruffled my hair. I jerked my head away but he didn't notice. "Where is everybody?" he asked and slid into a booth.

"How should I know?" I leaned on my broom and gave him a look.

"Whoa, Nelly," he said. "Guess someone got up on the wrong side of the bed."

Pfft! In the story of my life I was just going to delete him. I left and headed for the back, but stopped when I saw my mother.

She was standing in the kitchen looking out through the window in the door. She reached up, fixed her hair, took a deep breath, and plastered on a smile.

She poured him a cup of coffee and when she turned to go, he grabbed her ass. She giggled and flicked her rag at him pretending not to like it. It was an embarrassing display and they repeated the idiotic antic right in front of me. It made me want to kill myself, but it got my mother a twenty-dollar tip on a cup of coffee.

This triggered in Arlene a hot flash so enormous an audible sizzle of steam rose off her when she hit the cold air of the walk-in refrigerator.

Arlene had separated from her husband again. She was having trouble paying her rent and her hot flashes had gotten worse. They now included full-blown anxiety attacks and one or more of the following: aching joints, muscle pain, bouts of rapid heartbeat, bloating, itchy, crawly skin, and tingling extremities. All of them, apparently ("God help me!" Peter Pam had said), common symptoms of menopause.

When Arlene stepped out, it was clear the refrigerator had done little to cool her. Her eyes were shooting flames. Droplets of sweat beaded on her scalp through her thinning hair. She stormed right up to my mother and demanded a 50 percent cut of Vick's tip. "I'm the head waitress here and we're now pooling our tips, so fork it over." Peter Pam and I were sitting facing out at the empty counter. My mother and Arlene stood right in front of us. They'd been bickering for weeks about who got which tables and how many.

"Breathe through it," Peter Pam instructed me, closing her eyes, inhaling and exhaling. She'd been trying to teach me the art of "calmness," but the lesson wasn't working. My mother hissed at Arlene and I bit my fingernails until they bled. And when Arlene reached for my mother's apron pocket, their shouting erupted into a windmill of slapping.

"Bravo!" Peter Pam sprang to her feet. They stopped and looked at her, confused. "What folly!" She turned toward each one of them with prim little claps.

"Bravo!" she hollered again. "The denouement was simply splendid. And the dialogue was spot-on, spot-on!"

Peter Pam believed that the soul was almond shaped. I had always imagined a kidney bean, plump and red. "One thing I know for sure," she'd said to me, "it is not edible. It is solid like a rock. No matter what storm tries to capsize it, it simply laughs it off. The more you know of it, the more life reveals itself to be a farce."

My mother and Arlene looked at Peter Pam, stunned. "Now go on, the both of you. Off to your dressing rooms." She shooed them with the back of her hand. "Chop, chop." She clapped twice. In their confusion they stumbled off.

Peter Pam winked at me. "You see," she said, blowing on her fingernails and polishing them on her dress, "that is how you do it."

Sniff, sniff. My mother twitched her nose. "Something smells clean and fresh in here," she said, stepping in the door. Life had plunged me headlong into a cleaning frenzy. The first one I'd ever had. While she was out with Vick, I was home plunging the toilet and sweeping up the dead. I scrubbed all the floors. I scoured the mold off the shower stall and polished the sink. I glued back all the missing tiles on the floor and painted over the food splatter behind the stove. I reorganized our closets and alphabetized our dwindling supply of food. I reinforced the leaky ceiling with double-thick cardboard, triple-thick garbage bags, and extra-strength duct tape. I cleared cobwebs from corners. Every speck of dust underneath the couch was gone. There wasn't a single spot I missed. Our house was now a model home. But no matter how much I fixed it up, the scent of disinfecting Lysol was all my mother ever noticed.

"Can you take your shoes off?" I asked.

She stopped abruptly, looked at me, decided I was joking, and gave a dismissive wave. "Oh," she snorted, as in *Why bother?* and then she proceeded to track in all this mud.

We were losing the house anyway, she'd told me. So she abandoned it. Every time we got a letter from the bank, she tossed it out. She stopped doing her dishes and throwing her garbage away. She dropped her wrappers on the floor and left food out to spoil. I now trailed behind her with a rag, wiping up her mess.

I had just finished bleaching the linoleum but she walked across it and grabbed a handful of Ritz crackers. Every time she ate, all I saw were crumbs. They fanned out from her mouth in every direction, ricocheting when they hit the ground. Still chewing, she flopped down in the middle of the couch. She now did this any old time she pleased, never acknowledging that the only reason she could was because I had cleared it off. And I'd scrubbed out all the stains with high-octane spot remover too.

"I'm thinking about taking up yoga," she announced. I had no comment. I officially did not recognize her anymore. "There isn't anything yoga can do that a good fuck and a shot of bourbon can't do better," she'd claimed on more than one occasion.

"Lynette did yoga, did I tell you that?"

"Lyn who?" I asked.

She looked at me incredulously. "You know, Lyn-*ette*," as if simply repeating the name would clear things up. "As in *vinaigrette* and *kitchen dinette*? Vick said yoga really slimmed her down."

"Was she heavy?" I asked.

"No, not at all!" she retorted as if my conclusion was outrageous. "She was gorgeous. I stole a picture of her—do you want to see?"

Vick, she finally explained, producing a wallet-size photo from her bag, was a widower and Lynette was his dead wife. In the picture she was at the beach wearing a bikini, sitting on a towel, her legs pushed together, bracing herself on one arm. With her sunglasses pulled halfway down her nose, she gazed at the camera and smiled.

"She died in a boating accident. Can you imagine?" My mother wiped a speck of dust off the photo with her thumb. "It's so tragic."

Oh, please! I thought to myself. The official story was that Lynette slipped on something and her feet went out from under her.

Vick was a pitiful man. He was the kind of guy who had no idea how to catch or throw a ball. He probably tripped on his own feet and when he reached to steady himself on her, he accidentally pushed her overboard. And I was sure he didn't know how to swim. I imagined him immobilized and whimpering like a baby while his wife flailed and drowned.

My mother put the picture of Lynette back in her bag, reached across the couch to the side table, and helped herself to a Kleenex as if by magic the box had been neatly placed right there for her. "Poor Vick." She blew her nose. She picked up the pillow from the corner of the couch where I'd propped it up just so, and hugged it to her chest. She redid her hair clip at the back of her head and when she raised her arms her Kleenex fell.

Every time she was in the house, she messed it up again. She'd use the bathroom and leave the sink smeared with toothpaste. She'd change her clothes and drop them on the floor. And when she got home, she never noticed that they were neatly folded and replaced again.

Lynette, she continued, had been a woman of many hobbies. She sewed, she cooked, she played golf. My mother went on and on and with each hobby she listed, she tossed the pillow between her hands, spinning it in the air. Watching it made me dizzy.

I felt queasy now all the time anyway. My cleaning products gave me headaches. And the way my mother acted made me sick. Every topic she brought up was related to Vick. Mostly she talked about his house: it was so big, his things were so nice, the yard was so neat, and he had a pool. "A pool, Ruthie! Can you imagine that?" She went on and on. And she'd cleaned herself up in a way I really didn't care for. Her hair was always neat; she now ironed her clothes. She kept open fashion magazines on the edge of the bathroom sink so when she did her face for him it was a major production, not her usual effortless routine.

With Vick she became girly and stupid as if an idiotic twin had supplanted her. She didn't swear around him because she sensed he didn't like it. And apparently her twin had hearing loss. I tried once at work to tell her she had toilet paper stuck to her shoe, but she brushed right by me with Vick's plate of food, eager to serve him while it was still hot.

And now there was this Lynette! When she finally finished listing off her hobbies, the pillow landed.

"I don't know, what do you think?" my mother asked. "Should I take up yoga or crocheting? Or should I do both?"

With the pillow now on her lap, she grabbed her bag and fished out her pack of Camels. When she took out a cigarette, bits of tobacco spilled everywhere.

"I knew a woman once who crocheted toilet-seat covers." She picked off the tobacco crumbs and one by one tossed them on the floor. "She sold them on the Interweb."

And with that she gave the pillow a swipe with the back of her hand and the pillow landed on the floor. I was just about to scoop it up, brush it off, and restore it to its place at the corner of the couch when I heard a noise. My mother heard it too.

We looked at each other in silence waiting for it again. Then there it was: the unmistakable squeaking of a mouse. It stumbled out from the wall; a dusting of poison powdered its minuscule snout.

"For fuck's sake," my mother said, finally sounding more like herself. She stood up, walked over to the wall, and picked up the tennis racket she now used to kill them.

It was afternoon. The sun was bright. I had just cleaned the windows. And the light poured in at a brand-new angle. But she would never notice.

She raised the racket. "I can't wait to get out of this shithole," she said. And leaving the impression of tightly woven plaid, she smashed the mouse dead.

My mother later told me my face turned a shade of green and that she reached out with the tennis racket to break my fall. What I remembered next was waking up in bed with her sitting beside me. She held my hand and stroked my forehead. "You really scared me," she said. She took my temperature. She brought me water. She heated up some Campbell's soup. And when I was done with that, she popped a big bag of popcorn and got into bed with me. We watched reruns of *Star Trek* and cracked up over how boyish and stupid the show was. "Beam me up, Scotty," my mother mocked in a deep voice. When she threw a handful of popcorn at the screen, I didn't care that it landed on the floor. All I did was laugh.

I told myself she'd grow tired of him. I imagined her fixing her makeup, getting ready to break up with him. "His aftershave stinks! His dandruff is gross!" she'd jeer. I could just see her ducking in and out of the bathroom with each exclamation of disbelief. And I pictured the two of us howling.

My mother took my temperature one more time. I thought for sure she'd stay home with me, but at seven P.M. sharp she got up. She took a shower. She changed her clothes. I heard the familiar clatter as she pulled her makeup out and chucked it back into her bag.

"I gotta go." She was sitting on the edge of the bed again. I couldn't look at her. She reached to touch my cheek and I turned away.

Vick was old enough to be my mother's father and just the kind of man she claimed she'd never like.

"Ruthie," my mother pleaded. She kissed my shoulder. "Everything is going to be okay. I promise."

But I had never been so unsure.

CHAPTER TWENTY-SIX

Loyalty

The April of my junior year, I wrote a paper: *"Jesus Has Been Co-Opted by the Devil: An Examination of How the Perversion of His Teachings Is Destroying the World."*

I thought it was my best, but my teacher, Ms. Simmons, didn't even read it. She claimed that my subject matter had become "too dark."

Ms. Simmons was not the brightest bulb. Her face was thin and elongated and her features seemed crowded for room, so who knows, maybe she'd been squeezed in some elevator doors and suffered brain damage as a kid.

To humor her, I took my paper back and wrote about something more cheery: the Easter Bunny. And I tried a new angle—instead of just putting my thoughts down, I posed a series of questions. "Would Jesus think the Easter Bunny is doing a good job of representing his values? Through the mere existence of the Easter Bunny, is Jesus trying to tell us something? And if so, what would that be? That life makes perfect sense or that it's a ludicrous joke?" At this point in my paper,

Ms. Simmons had circled *Easter Bunny* several times, drawn a happy face, and written in the margin: "I already like this paper much better!"

✧

By the spring of 2008 business at Tiny's had slowed so much, Mel had Peter Pam pumping gas part-time (you can only imagine how it was ruining her nails) and I hardly ever saw her.

Vick Ward became Tiny's only regular customer. He was there every Saturday. He'd sip a cup of coffee for hours, grabbing at my mother and starting conversations. He had no clue that none of us liked him. We found out that he'd written the Hansons' loan and Patti and Roger's, too. His company had filed for bankruptcy but somehow they reorganized and Vick got promoted. He was now some kind of executive VP.

Arlene kept her eye on him. Just a look from her was enough to make him squirm.

One day she and I were standing up against the wall. He sat in the booth right across from us, waiting for his breakfast. "They're all pigs, assholes, greedy pricks." Arlene was going off on her new favorite topic: bankers and politicians. She was talking to me but looking at him. He stared out the window and pretended not to hear her. He shifted in his seat. "No, you know what they are? They're all a bunch of *thieves!*" Arlene spit the word at him and he flinched.

Just then, my mother came bounding through the kitchen door with Vick's hash browns. She was the only one who liked him. According to her, Vick had no idea the loans he made were bad, but Arlene and I did not believe it. We did not see him losing his house.

Vick looked up at my mother with a big smile and as soon as she put his plate down, he grabbed her and sat her on his lap. She now did this anytime he wanted her to. I tried not to watch, but I couldn't get over what she was doing. And she didn't care who saw it.

My mother tossed her head back and let out a giggle so high-pitched and phony, it left a stench in the air.

Even Arlene was impressed. "I might think he's a son of a bitch, but damn if she isn't good. I've never seen a girl work a man quite like that before."

Then, suddenly, because he wanted to, he pulled her into him and they started slobbering all over each other like a couple of loose-lipped monkeys.

It was so gross, I just couldn't help myself. I burst through the kitchen doors and dove for the sink, barely making it before I puked. And the next thing I knew, the floor was coming at me and I was leading with my head. Just before I hit the ground, *whoosh!* Arlene swooped up behind me. She caught me by my waist and sat me on a chair.

"Here, sweetheart, have some juice." And as if by magic she produced a glass. She moved closer and looked at my face. Her eyes were warm and brown.

Her only son had died overseas in the first Iraqi war. Peter Pam had made us swear we'd never breathe a word of it. The mere mention of it could send Arlene reeling off the edge. But I could see then in the tender way she looked at me that her son still lived on inside her.

She brushed a hair off my sweaty forehead. "You have always been a string bean, but you're getting way too thin." She cupped my chin. "Now drink up." She stood back, folded her arms, and waited to see how the juice went down.

"You see," she said after I took a sip, "you're more resilient than you think."

✧

On a Saturday morning when the restaurant had emptied out, Peter Pam and I were cleaning up. She finally had a shift inside the restaurant and was gleefully wiping down her tables, lip-synching with a ketchup bottle to Aretha Franklin on the stereo: "*R-E-S-P-E-C-T! Find out what it means to me!*"

With his arms stretched out over the top of the booth and a toothpick dangling in the corner of his mouth, Vick digested his food. He was the only customer left.

When he looked over at Peter Pam, he chuckled. And even though he was probably enjoying her performance—Peter Pam was that good—I took my apron off, balled it up, slapped it on the counter, and headed for his table. I wanted him to leave. I couldn't stand him. He didn't know it but my mother's relationship with him would never last. She hated men like him, finicky and picky about their clothes. And I could just tell, he had no idea how to change his oil or fix a leaky faucet.

I grabbed for his mug, but he stopped me.

"Whoa there, kid-o." He covered my hand over the top of the cup. "I'm still drinking that."

I looked down at his hand. He wore a ruby-studded pinky ring. His fingernails were polished, his palms soft and clammy.

I pulled at the mug but he pulled it back.

"I never noticed," he said, "but you got your mother's pretty eyes." He smiled and his eyes twinkled like a pair of artificial gems. I pushed my glasses up. For a moment I was afraid to move.

A reassuring hand touched my back.

"Will there be anything else today?" Mel said, reaching past me, filling Vick's water glass.

Vick let go of my hand on his mug.

"That's it," he said. "Say, what'd you put in those eggs today? They were extra good."

Mel ignored the compliment. He slid the check across the table. "Then you can settle up with me."

CHAPTER TWENTY-SEVEN

Guardian

Days went by. My mother dated Vick tirelessly and my mood worsened. She and I fought all the time. One night she emerged from the bathroom all dressed up for a date. She flung her arms out and flopped down on the couch. Her pocketbook in her outstretched hand hit the cushion with a thump.

"I'll have you know," she said, sticking her nose in the air all smug, "he's working on another loan for us."

"Why? Because the first one worked out so well?" I couldn't help myself. It was breathtaking how stupid she could be. We'd gotten caught up in a nationwide scam and she refused to see it. She grabbed her purse and stood up. "At least he's trying to get us out of this mess. What the fuck are you doing about it except hanging out with that tired old queen?" She stormed out and slammed the door behind her.

No matter how she sometimes hurt me or how hard I tried not to, I missed her when she was gone. When she was out, I hardly slept. I'd wait up and listen for the sound of a car, then her keys in the door. Her purse would hit the counter. She might open the freezer, pull the ice cream out, and eat it standing up. I'd hear the spoon clink against the bottom of the sink when she was done. Sometimes she took a shower. Sometimes she just slipped into bed. And I wouldn't move. I'd wait until I heard her breathing slow and then I'd inch my way onto my elbows to look at her, her mouth at rest, her lips slightly parted. I'd watch her chest rise and fall and listen to the rhythm of her sleeping. It wasn't until I knew for certain that she was home and next to me that I could close my eyes and rest.

I looked around our house. I was desperate not to lose it. But the truth was, it wasn't this house that mattered, it was her. She was the only thing that kept me from slipping through the cracks.

She'd started staying out all night with him, so now I never slept. I paced around the house cleaning things.

That night around ten, I thought I heard a car door slam so I looked out the window, but there was nothing. Miss Frankfurt must have heard the noise too because she was standing in her window peering out with Patti and Roger's binoculars. She now owned them. She'd bought them at their last tag sale. And she used them to follow my mother's every move. She'd watch my mother go, and Miss Frankfurt's lights wouldn't go out until she confirmed my mother was home again.

That night, her binoculars wandered all around. When they landed on me, she lowered them.

Ten minutes later, Pancake started barking his high-pitched frantic yelp, a particular bark that meant one thing: Miss Frankfurt was stepping out. And sure enough when I looked out the window again, she was closing her door. She stood on the top step, adjusted her hat, and took a deep inhale as if summoning the courage to move forward.

It was spring. The days were warm and the nights were perfect for sleeping. My life was falling apart but the weather had been glorious and the contrast irked me to no end.

But that night there wasn't anything else you could see but beauty. The atmosphere was an iridescent regal blue. A million stars shimmered and pulsed in the sky as if it were breathing. Rapture seemed to be upon us and it was impossible not to feel swept up in its embrace.

When Miss Frankfurt reached the end of her walkway, she pointed herself in my direction and started moving again. The full weight of her waddled from one leg to another. She carried an orange beach bag. The moonlight grazed the shoulders of her light-blue coat. Her arms swung at her sides laboriously as if bringing them along strained her. And even though she huffed and puffed and her hat almost fell off twice, there was something about her that fit the splendor of the night. In Miss Frankfurt there was an unquestionable queen, and that queen was heading right toward me. So I did what my instincts told me to: I hid.

She rang the bell, didn't wait a split second, then rang it again. "I know you're in there, I just saw you, so open up."

When I did, she pushed past me with her beach bag and urgently pulled out a kitchen chair. With a moan of relief, she sat herself down at the table. She caught her breath, took off her jacket, and settled it onto the back of her chair. She removed a hankie from her sleeve just as I imagined Jane Austen would.

"Well," she said, dabbing her brow, "don't just stand there, get me a glass of water."

I moved quickly. "Here." I set a glass down in front of her, stole my hand away, and stepped back.

"For God's sake, I don't bite," she said.

She picked up the water and guzzled it. Then she started again, dabbing the back of her neck.

When she caught my eye, she stopped. "Sit, sit," she insisted, gesturing with her hankie at the chair across from her.

Her straw hat was decorated with fake flowers and twigs. A few bumble bees were sprinkled about. It seemed like an entire patch of earth had just been tossed onto her head. And the whole arrangement looked as if it needed watering, but she unpinned it from her head and placed it on the table with utmost care.

"Now," she sighed. Her hazel eyes pooled at the bottom of her thick glasses. She tucked the hankie back into her sleeve. "Let me make sure we have everything we need." She leaned to one side, reached into the beach bag, and without breaking her lopsided pose pulled out a pad of paper and pen. Every move she made took effort. Then, as if it weighed a ton, she hefted out a box, and—*thud!*—dropped it on the table.

Scrabble! it said in script.

"If you don't know it, I'll teach you," she said.

According to Miss Frankfurt, she'd never played with anyone who caught on so quickly. Halfway through game one, we put away the dictionary. By game two we were playing without the timer. She was impressed with all my moves. Two hours went by, but it felt like ten minutes. We used all our brain power, scheming so we barely spoke. I came within points of beating her.

Then she folded up the board and returned it to her bag. "Well," she said. "I've got to put my feet up. These dogs of mine are howling. But let me tell you something. I had a talk with that teacher of yours. She'd complained about your papers. She's lucky I didn't fire her."

She pulled her glasses down and the blurry puddles of washed-out color at the bottom of her lenses brightened into light green jewels. She moved forward and looked into me as if she were seeing my soul.

"Any fool can tell by the way you frame your arguments: there is greatness in you. And you should know it."

Miss Frankfurt made her way home in the same labored fashion, the indelible blue of her coat flickering behind her as she went. A few minutes later her den light went on where I imagined her settling back down with her book.

CHAPTER TWENTY-EIGHT

Persistence

I came home from school to find my mother spread-eagle on our bed. She had separators in between her newly polished toes. Her face was coated with a teal-colored facial mask. What I thought were cucumber slices covered her eyes, but on closer examination I realized they were zucchinis. (They were on sale, she explained later.) Her lips were the only thing that weren't a shade of green. They were plumped up and red, gleaming with eucalyptus-smelling gloss.

"Mom?"

She didn't move.

It was hard to tell if she was breathing so I leaned in and took a closer look. A reflection of myself towered over her in the sheen of her mask.

"What are you staring at?" she said.

I stood up, startled. Her mouth hadn't even moved! "Aren't you supposed to be at work?" I asked.

She mouthed something that I couldn't understand.

"What?"

She said it again.

"What?" I repeated.

"For Chrissake, Ruthie!" she bolted upright and the zucchinis fell. "Can't you see? I'm resting! Oh, never mind." She got up and pushed by me.

"I thought you were working today." I followed her into the bathroom.

"I'm sick of that place. And I'm tired of everyone there."

She went on, but I stopped listening. She was splashing her face with water. Green goo was flying everywhere and I had just cleaned the bathroom. "And look at this place," she said. She flung her hands up and a spray of it hit the wall. "It's so dreary and small."

A glob flew upward. For a moment it held its shape and hovered in the air. Then, *bam!* It dropped and splattered all over the floor.

She picked up a towel, dampened a corner, and started scouring her face. It was going to take me forever to clean up this mess. In an act of total desperation I grabbed her towel, threw myself down, and started mopping.

"What the hell is wrong with you?" She gave me a little kick when I didn't respond. "Look at me!" she demanded. I stopped and looked up. Her hair was twisted in a white rag. The front of her bathrobe was open. There was still a thin line of green at the edge of her face so it looked as if she were wearing a mask of herself.

"You gotta stop this, Ruthie. Life moves on and we were fools to think our luck would last."

We had been here before, teetering on the edge of homelessness. She'd fall into a predictable pattern of drinking and napping. Any state of consciousness in between would set her on edge. I don't know how she mustered the will to keep going, but she always did. She'd get out of bed, reel in her drinking, touch up her nails, color her hair, and exfoliate her skin. She'd look around to see which man she could blow. Or which one might save us. It filled me with dread and sadness, but it was too painful for her to see.

She raised her head and cinched her robe. "Now get up off the floor." She clenched her jaw and stepped by me.

CHAPTER TWENTY-NINE

Reality

P eter Pam bought me "green" cleaning products and gave me an old upright Hoover she'd found standing in someone's trash. Mel fixed it up. He touched up the paint and polished the chrome. He carried it in his arms up our walkway and presented it to me as if it were a bride. "Isn't she a beaut?" He set her down, unwound the cord from the neck, and demonstrated how she worked. "She's got a high and low beam and her wheels pivot, making it easy to navigate in all directions." And with one easy tap of a foot control, he showed me how to secure the handle upright and set her into park. It was awesome.

But in mid-May, it poured. The leak broke through our ceiling, the cardboard hinged open like a door. A gush of dirty water spanked my linoleum. Bits of ceiling plaster flew everywhere and a dead squirrel—*thwack, thwack*—bounced off the counter and landed on the floor. Like a volunteer fire department, Peter Pam and Mel showed up without my asking with a piece of plywood and a screw gun, but life was falling down around me and nothing could keep it up.

✦

My mother took me for a drive. She wouldn't tell me where we were going.

"You'll see," she said. "Besides, you could use some fresh air."

We were heading in the direction of Walmart, but then she turned. She stepped on the gas and pulled onto the highway.

She and I barely saw each other anymore and when we did, we hardly spoke. When we slept together we didn't spoon, and half the time one of us would end up sleeping on the couch.

But the highway always brought us back again.

My mother turned up the radio and went faster. We opened our windows. The landscape widened and the sky stretched on forever.

On the highway, life's possibilities were easy to imagine. I looked out the window and saw a motorcade escorting us along. A whole new life projected on the road. One that included incredible things. For example, lunch with Hillary Clinton. In the reflection of the windshield, I saw us at a table enjoying Diet Cokes.

My mother sat forward and turned up the volume.

"These boots are made for walking"—she looked at me and smiled. This was one of her favorite songs. She swayed and snapped her fingers.

The day was warm and long. The trees were full. The sun shined through the leaves and left brushstrokes of yellow on the earth. Wildflowers—purples and saffrons, oranges and blues—stippled the edge of the road. One day the planet might be too hot for anything to blossom, but that day, it was hard to imagine.

My mother was really hamming it up, slapping the steering wheel. *"One of these days these boots are going to walk all over you!"* She galloped in her seat and her voice went low. Moments like this were all we had, so I let myself go and the two of us laughed.

✧

An hour later, she shook me awake. "Here we are," she sang. I had fallen asleep and in that time, her fake, cheerful twin had come back. I could tell by the way she was sitting upright in her seat. She turned left, she turned right. She turned left, she turned right. Each time she was careful to come to a full stop and use her blinker—two things I'd never seen her do before.

"Isn't it beautiful?" she asked.

I looked around. We were driving through the center of a town. The houses lined the streets in even rows.

"And"—she rounded the corner onto Center Street—"you're not going to believe this, but"—she pulled to a stop—"there's a Starbucks!"

"Are you high?" I couldn't help but ask. She and I were Dunkin' Donuts girls through and through.

She put the car in park, tapped me on the knee, and said, "Oh," as in, *Oh, don't be silly.* "I'm going to go grab an iced chai latte, do you want one?" She sprang out of the car.

Across the street, an orchestra was getting ready to give a concert on the green. The audience sat in white folding chairs waiting, I imagined, for something cheerfully baroque. The green was dotted with tender saplings perched on mounds of ochre-colored mulch, as if they'd been dropped neatly into place that morning. The sky above was primary blue. A cute puffy cloud went by, giving the scene just the right touch of ironic fake realism.

"I knew you'd like it here," my mother said, ducking back into the car with her latte.

"I have no idea where we are."

"This is Westland," she said.

"Wasteland?"

"No, Westland," she repeated, "as in north and south. You know, Westland, where Vick lives."

They'd changed the rules, she told me, and the loan Vick was working on for us hadn't gone through. The bank would kick us out soon. So, she said, "We're moving in with him."

She always did this. If she was afraid to tell me something, she'd just slip it into a conversation and act as if it were a given truth. I could tell by the way she was innocently scratching her cheek that she was hoping she'd gotten away with it. But I shot her one of my most melodramatic looks of disgust. I twisted my features as much as possible and, in case she needed help seeing it, I thrust the expression at her and flew out the door.

Fat River was the only place I ever loved and no one was going to take that away from me.

Ta-da-da-da. Ta-da-da-da. Suddenly there was music.

The first few notes of Beethoven's Fifth thundered out from the orchestra as I stormed along the shoulder of the road.

Mel had told us we could move back behind the gas station if we lost the house. My mother wouldn't hear of it though. She was sick and tired of living so close to the edge. But I didn't care about her anymore. I decided right then and there, I was going to live in the gas station without her.

My mother pulled the car back onto the street and stepped lightly on the gas to follow me.

An empty paper cup crossed my path. I stepped on it, delighted by the *crunch*.

Peter Pam and I had already measured the space. She had all sorts of decorating ideas. "A nice braided rug would brighten and warm the place right up," she'd told me.

"Ruthie!" my mother called. "What are you doing?" She was steering with one hand and shouting at me over the seat through the open passenger-side window.

There was a patch of dirt behind the station where Arlene said there used to be tomatoes so I could have my own garden.

"Get back in the car!" my mother shouted.

The violin section played furiously. They jerked their heads, they snapped their strings. At the end of every riff, in a wild madcap gesture, they flung their bows toward the sky.

I sped up. My mother did too. This time when she caught up with me, she stopped and got out of the car. "I mean it, Ruthie," she screamed over the roof. "If you don't get back in this instant, I'll leave without you!"

"Pffft!" I sputtered. *See if I care!* Then I flipped my fingers under my chin like I was Italian.

A woman across the street gaped at us and drew her Williams-Sonoma shopping bag closer in. I walked faster. My mother got back in the car, pulled forward, got out again, and assumed the same position at her door.

"What's that supposed to mean?" she yelled, but I didn't answer.

This time when she got back in the car and stepped on the gas, the wheels spun.

This prompted a loud gasp from the two women now watching us.

"You know, you can be a real a-hole!" My mother was out of the car again yelling. "For the first time in, oh, let me think—" I stopped, jabbed my fists on my hips and glared at her like, *This should be good!*

She had propped up her elbow with her hand and was tapping her finger to her lips, looking up in a mock thinking pose. "My entire life!" she yelled. "I've cleaned up my act and finally gotten us a decent place to live and this is how you thank me?

"And another thing . . ." She tore her bag off her shoulder, dug out a pack of cigarettes, and pawed at them madly. One after another, cigarettes spilled out and broke. "You think I'm stupid, don't you?" She finally managed to get a whole cigarette out and shoved it into her mouth. "Well, let me tell you something." The unlit cigarette quaked, then she removed it and yelled, "I'm not!" and put it back again.

Her new haircut indicated otherwise. It was shoulder length on one side, cropped on the other in an asymmetrical look that just screamed *Idiot!* to me.

"I know exactly what you're trying to do. But I am not going to let it happen. Nope!" When she jerked her head only half her hair swayed.

She fished out her lighter from her bag, sparked a flame, lit her cigarette, and, without thinking about what she was doing, she slammed the lighter down on the ground and lurched toward me. "Not this time!" she barked. "There is no fucking way I'm going to let you talk me out of this one."

A small group of women had gathered across the street gawking at us as if they'd unwittingly been sucked into a bad made-for-TV movie.

The street behind them was lined with shops that looked as if they'd been pressed in molds like candies and the row of tulips along the sidewalk exuded an unnaturally high wattage of color. God had turned up the contrast on life and dropped me into a badly sculpted play set.

The only thing that looked real was the ash on the tip of my mother's cigarette. She moved the cigarette to her mouth. She inhaled. A line of smoke spiraled up, the ash grew longer, and a sprinkle of it drifted to the ground.

"He not only owns a house with a pool, it has three bathrooms! Count them!" She shoved three fingers in my face and wiggled them. With the cigarette she pointed to the tips of each one. "One, two . . ." She enunciated the words slowly like a nursery school teacher, but her hands shook like a hard-edged old lady's. The ash hung by a thread. An explosion of percussions boomed across the green. "Three!" My mother touched her last fingertip, Beethoven's Fifth crescendoed, and the ash fell. In my head, when it hit the ground a mushroom cloud erupted. A blast of radioactive dust smacked the ground and obliterated the planet.

In the space that followed, a dead silence hushed across the green like snow. For a moment the audience sat awestruck. The women across the street held their breath. My mother inhaled and a brand-new ash sizzled.

I cleared my throat. I blinked. "Mel said he'd put in a new shower stall."

"Encore!" the audience clapped and shouted.

My mother's shoulders dropped. "Ruthie." She sighed, as in *Don't be so naïve.*

"Delete, delete, delete," a bird in the sapling nearest us chirped.

"Please," my mother said. Her tone had softened. The women across the street moved onward. The sun angled downward.

"Please, Ruthie. He has a washing machine and a dryer and a dishwasher that works. The plumbing doesn't clatter and not a single window is broken. And I'm tired." Her bottom lip began to quiver, but I told myself I didn't care. "I just need a place to rest."

I took a deep breath. I felt my insides soften.

She was only thirty-two, but the weight of a hundred hard lifetimes was etched across her face. Last winter's cough had never fully gone away. The rattle in her lungs had worsened. And no amount of makeup could cover the heavy darkness that had settled beneath her eyes.

My mother began to weep. She dropped her head and her shoulders shook. I could see the winged bones of her back beneath the thin fabric of her dress. A length of hem hung below her knees, weighted down by the safety pin that had held it up for days.

"Don't cry," I said. When my mother cried, nothing else existed but her sadness, and her sadness ran so deep that if I didn't stop it, it would drown us both.

She raised her head and looked at me. A well of wounded dreams shimmered at the bottom of her eyes.

"Don't cry," I said again. I reached out and took her hand. "Everything will be okay, I promise."

"The summer, Ruthie, that's all I'm asking, so I can catch my breath. And after that, if it doesn't work out, we'll move back."

A breeze kicked up. The leaves on the trees fluttered and a netting of light flickered across the road. A flock of birds cut across the sky and drew a curtain on the sun.

"I promise," she said.

When I thought about hell, I thought about life without my mother. She was all I ever really had. I tried to picture who I'd be without her and the only image that came to mind was of a ghost.

CHAPTER THIRTY

Farewell

"Relax and drop your shoulders," Peter Pam said to me. We were sitting cross-legged on a pair of oversize pillows on the floor in her apartment.

Peter Pam's apartment was like a womb. Maroon Indian-print fabric was stapled to the walls. Plumes of it bloomed off the ceiling.

Life was crashing down on me and there was nothing I could do but watch it happen. I'd given up on our house. I now balled my trash up and chucked it on the floor. Sometimes I'd pick it up just for the satisfaction of throwing it down again. Once, on my way to the kitchen table I dropped a bowl of cereal and instead of cleaning it up, I took my foot and ground each bit of it into the linoleum. It had taken me months and months to get our house fixed up and—*snap!*—just like that, it was trash again.

"Now close your eyes," Peter Pam said, "and think about nothing."

What was nothing? What did it look like and how did it smell? My mind was prone to wander, asking unanswerable questions until I wanted to shoot myself, but the sound of Peter Pam's voice calmed me.

"See yourself standing at the top of a mountain. The sky is all around you. A breeze grazes your cheek."

I began to see the place clearly. I was in the Alps somewhere. I looked around me. A smattering of wildflowers bloomed in between patches of melting snow.

"You take in a full breath of crystal-clear air. Your heart rate drops."

I saw myself from above standing at the highest place on earth. I widened my stance, opened my arms, arched back, and looked up as if to say to God, *Here I am. I am right here.*

Something touched my cheek and eased me back into the room. Peter Pam slowly filled my vision. She was shaking me. "Rooster," she said. Rooster was the nickname she used for me in urgent situations.

"Rooster!" *Snap snap!* Her two fingers appeared in front of my face as I came to.

"Oh, thank the Lord." She patted her chest. "What happened to you?"

"I don't know," I said. "It was weird."

"You had this look on your face like you were never coming back. It scared me." She pulled me into her. The stuffing in her bra crackled. Then suddenly she pushed me back. "You weren't messing with me, were you?" She lowered her eyes, cocked her head, and studied me.

"No," I said. "I don't know what happened but it felt as if I slipped through time."

"Wow." Her face softened. She let go of my shoulders, sat back against the wall, and settled me in her arms again.

"What was it like?" she asked after a while.

"It was beautiful."

She scrunched us closer together.

A long soothing silence swaddled us. Dave jumped up, circled Peter Pam's lap, and made himself a bed. Peter Pam caressed him with long, wistful, head-to-tail strokes.

"You know what I think?" she finally said. "I think the meaning of life is this."

"What?"

"This." She raised her hand and drew the universe with her finger. Then she pointed back and forth from me to her to Dave. "This," she said again.

I sighed and smiled at her. I closed my eyes and rested there. Dave began to purr.

If I never made another friend, I wouldn't care.

"You'll be all right." She tilted my head back and kissed my forehead. "I know you will."

We left Fat River on a Sunday morning in June 2008. By then our electricity had been cut off and an eviction notice had been taped to our door.

Early that morning before the restaurant opened, Arlene threw a party. It was a sad little gathering that wasn't much fun. To begin with, Tiny's petty cash was almost gone so Arlene had to get a discounted day-old cake. It said "HAPPY 90th LARRY!" on it. According to Arlene, the cake was half off because the girl behind the counter told her that the very moment the baker finished the exclamation mark, Larry croaked. None of us knew

Larry, but we were in mourning anyway. Even Mel—the most even-tempered person I'd ever met—sat down and joined in our sadness.

My mother wasn't there. She claimed she had too much packing to do, though her stuff had been packed and ready weeks ago. She and Arlene were barely speaking anyway. She was through with Peter Pam and she told herself that Mel was just like every other boss she'd had: a real prick.

When my mother pulled up to get me, she turned the car around so it faced the street. She sat there idling, low in the seat, in an extra-big pair of sunglasses as if she were afraid to be seen.

"Think of it like a summer vacation," Arlene said, patting my hand.

"And you can always come back," Mel added.

I slid out of the booth. I knew this episode with Vick would never last. I gave it only weeks before my mother started hating him. But when Arlene and Mel pressed me in a hug between them, the lump in my throat grew so big I couldn't swallow.

Peter Pam and I told ourselves this wasn't good-bye. We would meet again. "I promise you," she said. My chin began to quiver.

"Now don't you start." She shook her finger. "You'll get me going." She dabbed at the corner of her eye with her pinky. "And my mascara will run."

I opened my mouth to say good-bye.

"Hup, hup." She pressed her finger to my lips. "Shh, I don't want to hear it. Now give me a hug." And she gathered me in her arms.

The three of them followed me out. Mel wheeled my bike up to the car. He had given me a bicycle rack, and he helped me put the bike on it. I got in the car and looked out the window. Under the flashing hot dog sign, like gracefully descending musical notes, they stood in order by height—Arlene, the tallest, Peter Pam, and then Mel. My mother stepped on the gas. They waved good-bye and in the dust that turned up behind us, they vanished.

My mother had spent months convincing herself she was done with Fat River. She'd claimed that when we left, she wouldn't miss a single thing. But I could see by the way she sat in her seat and stared at the road, that this was not entirely true.

I found out that year how her mother died. When I was cleaning out our closet, I discovered a newspaper clipping in an envelope among my mother's stuff.

There was a picture of her at age four, holding a teddy bear. She was wearing sandals and the sweetest little yellow dress I'd ever seen.

This little girl, the article said, was eating toast. Her mother was in her bathrobe, sipping coffee and, I imagined, smiling at her daughter across the kitchen table. Then her mother's boyfriend walked in, took out a gun, and shot her in the head. The shot was to the temple and knocked her off her seat. "The victim's daughter," the clipping read, "was in shock, but unharmed." The police found my mother quaking, still sitting at the table, staring at the blood splatter on her toast.

I looked over at my mother and saw that little girl. I wondered what happened to her shoes and that dress.

We left Fat River slowly, creeping along the familiar roads back to the highway.

Behind her sunglasses, my mother was crying. I reached across the seat and held her hand.

"Okay," my mother said, "enough of this." She wiped her face and sniffled. She tapped me on the thigh. "Now how about some music." She leaned forward and pushed in our favorite CD. But not even the best of seventies disco had the power to soothe us.

Part Three

CHAPTER THIRTY-ONE

Godforsaken

WELCOME! an oval sign exclaimed. The aggressively bold capital lettering made me feel the opposite.

Vick lived an hour away from Fat River in a subdivision called Piney Hills, but there was nothing piney or hilly about it. There were no trees and the earth had been flattened out into a smooth blanket of lawn. As we drove in, periscopes of gyrating water rose up from the ground to keep it green. Short fast arcs jetted back and forth, up and down the streets, timed, it seemed, to follow the sun.

My mother slowed to a crawl. "Isn't it nice?" she crooned. Our car was falling apart. It coughed and clanged and a line of smoke trailed behind us, but she sat upright grinning as if she were a diplomat in a Cadillac.

All of a sudden, *boom!* We hit a speed bump and she went flying. She smashed her head on the ceiling and the impact snapped her out of her reverie. "*Fuuuuuck!!*" she yelled. She slammed on the brakes and our pile of junk in the back landed on the floor. "God! Am I bleeding?"

She lowered her head and I parted her hair to examine her scalp.

"Nope."

She took a minute, twisted the rearview mirror, and brushed a strand of hair off her forehead. She turned her face and wiped something invisible from her cheek. Resuming her position in the seat, she cleared her throat and pulled forward.

The speed bump tore a hole in our muffler, but my mother didn't seem to notice.

"Look," she said, "there's a person!" A woman stood in front of her house. Her bright yellow dress clashed against the green of her lawn, flattening her shape and leaving a flaring at her edges as if someone had plugged her in.

"Wave," my mother said, and honked the horn. "Look!" She gawked out the window. "She's waving back."

But the woman wasn't waving. She was shielding her eyes, squinting into the sun.

"See how friendly people are around here?" My mother plumped herself up in the seat and picked up her cup of Diet Coke. With a long, loud, slurp she sucked the last sip through her straw, rattled the cup to confirm it was empty, then reached her hand out and dropped it on the street. I turned and looked behind me.

The woman covered her mouth and watched the cup tumble. It slid to a stop in a perfect landing, kick-standing on its straw. And just before we pulled around the corner, a crow swooped down on it as if he'd been waiting all his life for trash like us to litter.

✧

The entrance to Vick's driveway was flanked by pillars with stone squirrels perched on top. They clutched their acorns and eyed us as if we were thieves. His stucco McMansion shimmered on an expanse of lawn. It was totally gaudy, but my mother gazed up at it transfixed. "I told you it was beautiful."

We parked in the driveway and walked up a set of curved granite steps to his front door. The doorbell sang a tune with an authoritative tone that I really didn't care for, but the lyrics were brilliant: *ding-dong, ding-dong, ding-dong, ding-dong,* it chimed, perfectly identifying the homeowner.

Vick was almost fifty. His hair was slicked back into panels of glossy black, dipping and peaking like dunes. With his veneer of white teeth he reminded me of someone, but I wasn't able to put my finger on who it was. That day, when his oversize door slowly pulled open and the sticky heat outside collided with his central air, it was as if Vick emerged through dry ice. And I realized, *Oh my God! It's Liberace!*

I couldn't help myself. I bent over and chuckled into my hand.

Vick was just the kind of guy my mother used to laugh at. But this time she found nothing funny. She took her purse and swatted me. From her perspective, she'd hooked a big rich one and I had no appreciation for what she'd done.

He stood waiting, one hand on the doorknob, the other holding up a martini. "Come in, come in." He gestured flamboyantly with his glass.

My mother plastered on a smile. "Don't be rude," she said through her teeth. She walked by and as if to prove some point, she immediately started making out with him.

I stood in the foyer feeling awkward, looking up at the cathedral ceiling. A cut-glass chandelier twinkled in midair as if God had placed it precisely there.

"Ruthie!" Vick shouted, noticing me. It was grating how loud he could be. "I almost didn't recognize you without your baseball cap!" With his hand outstretched, he stepped closer to mess up my hair, but I pulled away from him.

"Gee whiz." He retreated. "Guess someone got up on the wrong side of the bed again, didn't she?"

It would never last here. Vick was an imbecile and if there was one thing my mother couldn't stand, it was infancy in men.

My mother flared her nostrils and glared at me. To annoy her, I grinned.

Vick went out and retrieved our things—my mother's old suitcase and three garbage bags full of stuff. As if he had no use for our shitty belongings, he dropped them in the foyer, then bellowed, "Let me give you a tour!" He shut the door. The weather stripping swept across the floor and the door sealed behind us. He headed down a hallway and we followed him.

His house smelled like scented candles. New antiques and fake cultural artifacts, the kind of things they make in China and sell at Crate and Barrel, adorned every room. There was an eerie echo in the house and an artificially pleasant light bounced off his objects, as if they were part of a *Desperate Housewives* stage set.

In front of us, Vick blathered on about the construction of the house—how long it took and what things were made of. The floors were oak, the tile in the kitchen was from Italy.

Every surface was accessorized with a pitcher or ceramic bowl. A giant rug hung down the wall of his staircase. "Blind orphans made this in Africa," my mother breathed, gently running her fingers over the surface of it. "Lynette bought it at Blooming-dale's." My mother raised her eyebrows as if this were actually the most interesting thing about it.

Stuff that people normally used—teacups and plates and pitchers—were imprisoned in china cabinets or sitting on shelves. The candles in the candelabra at the center of the dining-room table had never seen a flame.

"Don't touch that!" my mother warned when she glanced back and saw me pick up an apple from a bowl of wooden fruit. "It's decorative." This concept confused me. What was the purpose of having so much stuff if you weren't going to use it?

I followed my mother down another hallway. She paused a moment to graze her finger on the marble table along the wall. She contemplated the centerpiece—a boat-shaped bowl filled with black marbles—with an idiotic rapturous look on her face that annoyed me.

"Move it," I said, shoving her.

Vick finally led us to his living room.

"I just love this room." Shielding her mouth with her hand, my mother moved closer and whispered to me, "He reserves it for special occasions." One look around told me he didn't have many.

The furniture, the carpet, the walls, everything in it was white. The off-white crown molding looked bold in comparison. The floor-to-ceiling windows didn't open. Thin sheer drapes framed the windows, limp and motionless.

Two large fake-Japanese twig arrangements flanked a fireplace laid with decorative birch logs. A mirror hung above the mantel and reflected the pretentious artwork on the opposite wall: a light-beige square stenciled on a blank white canvas. *Oh, please!*

"Sit, sit. I've put out some cheese and crackers." Vick handed my mother a martini. She guided me behind the glass coffee table and sat us both down on the couch.

I'd never understood the ritual of drinks and hors d'oeuvres. What purpose did it serve? But my mother was performing masterfully. Perched on the edge of her seat, she daintily ate her cheese and crackers. She held her martini glass, pinkie extended, like Jackie Onassis would.

In my opinion, she was overdoing it. But Vick seemed completely fooled.

In his plaid shorts and pink oxford shirt, he stood across from us leaning against the mantel on his elbows. His stomach hung over his belt but his legs were like sticks. They made his tasseled loafers without socks seem huge on the ends of his ankles. I took note: I could easily push him over if I had to. He took his toothpick out of his mouth and in his overzealous thunderous tone immediately started bragging about his golf game.

Just this morning, he told us, he'd played his best ever. He then painstakingly recounted every shot, explaining his strategy and describing the trajectory of each one of his balls. With his new 5-iron, he'd hit a perfect approach shot on the ninth hole. He birdied twice. He used words like *back nine*, *bogey*, and *bite*, *short sticks* and *drivers*, *3-woods* and *putters*. It was exhausting to listen to. And even though my mother had no idea what he was talking about, she hung on his every word, shamelessly stroking his ego.

When I was seven, I stabbed a guy in the knee who was choking my mother. When I was eight, we were sleeping in some burnt-out building on a mattress on the floor and when I woke up face-to-face with a rat, I killed it with my bare hands. I took it by the tail and flung it up against the wall. When it quivered, I smashed it with a book.

But I couldn't stomach this. I looked up at the ceiling and tuned them out. *La-la-la-la*, I sang inside my head and let my mind wander.

Luckily I'd gotten to the point where I could conjure up Hillary Clinton anytime I wanted. It was early June and she'd just lost the nomination. I wondered, was she home in bed recuperating, or was she already at her desk planning her next move? Maybe she was out with Bill. Or maybe she was at the gym working off some steam. I liked the thought of her with Chelsea, the two of them curled up on the couch watching TV together. I saw myself sitting next to them. I leaned in and said something hysterical.

"Ruthie," my mother said.

Chelsea and Hillary both laughed. "You're so funny!" they howled.

"Ruthie." My mother knocked me on the shoulder.

She pointed and I realized Vick was standing there handing me a present. He crouched down right in front of me and shook the box slightly. "I think you're really going to like it," he said. When he winked at me, his smile broadened and filled my view.

I turned away and looked at my mother.

"Take it," she said, nodding and raising her eyebrows. She had one too. A box wrapped in the same paper sat on her lap. "He got it for you. Isn't that nice?"

Neither of them seemed to get that I wanted nothing to do with him.

"Here," he said. He set the box gingerly down on my lap and backed away.

My mother tore her package open first. "Oh my God," she shrieked, "it's Gucci!" and she jumped to her feet hugging her new bag.

She inhabited this new character of hers so completely, I found myself constantly looking around, searching for the movie lights. I half expected the walls to fall away and a new stage set to glide in. My mother had always hated Gucci, but when I opened my mouth to remind her, she threatened me with a glare.

"I love it." She stroked and posed it on her hip.

Vick smiled all proud of himself, and when she finished her display, he shifted his toothpick to the side of his mouth, took it out, and looked at me. "Go on," he said, raising the pick in my direction, "open yours."

So I did. The box, like my mother's, was from Neiman Marcus. I pried the top off and peeled the tissue paper back. What I really needed was a pair of jeans, but as I lifted it out, what unfurled in front of me was a dress.

My face turned red-hot. I dropped it on my lap.

"What's the matter?" he said. "Don't you like it?"

I did not wear dresses and anyone who knew me knew that. In my whole life I'd never worn a single one. I wore jeans and T-shirts only—short sleeves in the summer, long sleeves in the winter—and I liked them loose and big. My mother stood facing me, clutching the purse, not knowing what to do. I looked at her pleadingly, but all she did was stare back.

"Try it on," he said. "If it fits, I'll take you both to the country club for lunch."

My mother's eyes widened. She took a gulp of air, then pinched her lips to stifle her reaction. This time she wasn't faking it, I could tell.

"She'd love to!" she proclaimed. Before I could respond, she grabbed me by the wrist and towed me out.

"I'm not wearing that," I said to her.

"Please, Ruthie, you'll hurt his feelings."

"Like I care," I mumbled. "And besides, since when do you like Gucci?"

"People can change."

"Pfft," I sputtered. "Not *that* much."

"Why is it that you hate every guy who's nice to me?"

I had no comment.

"I mean it, I'd really like to know. He has just invited us to a *country club*," she enunciated as if I were stupid. "He's trying to be nice to you."

I did not budge. She was totally faking it here. It pained me to see her this way, making less of herself than she was. And she knew wearing a dress was a line I wouldn't cross.

She shifted her strategy. She put her hands together, knitted her brow with melodramatic sadness, and batted her eyes. "Pleeeease, Ruthie. It would mean so much to me."

I looked away. She could play these helpless female roles all she wanted.

"Ruthie, I'm asking you, look at me." She took my chin and turned my face. Her tone had softened. "Just once in my life before I die, I'd like to see the inside of a country club."

Sometimes who I was and what I wanted got lost when I was with her.

"Please . . . It would make me so happy."

I hated disappointing her and she knew that too.

"Oh, for Chrissake. Stop that," I said, and snatched the dress from her hand.

When she and I finally left this place, I would make her pay. I'd make her listen to nineties music in the car; I'd force her to watch *Grey's Anatomy* until she vomited.

CHAPTER THIRTY-TWO

Humiliation

Dear Lady Pam-o-lot,

Peter Pam and I promised we would write each other every week. We'd decided that in our letters this is what I'd call her. She'd address me as "My Dearest Cousin Ruth." We'd use pen and paper and stamps and we'd hone our arguments and philosophical musings with flowery language. Words like *whence* and *wherefore* would be sprinkled in throughout, Years from now someone might find our letters in an attic, and we were certain that feigning British nobility would only help to get them published.

I hate it here. Today Mother made me wear a dress. You cannot imagine how horrid it feels to me. I simply do not know how you do it.

Cheerio for now!
Your Dearest Cousin Ruth

P.S. I can't find my Tiny's baseball cap. Is it hanging on the hook by the back door?

I composed this letter in my head on the way through the country club parking lot. The dress was killing me. The hips were too tight. Every time I took a step, it corkscrewed up my waist. And I was wearing a pair of my mother's heels. Like a dog in boots, it simply did not seem right.

My mother took small quick steps in front of me. Her tight skirt truncated her stride. She'd touched up her nails in the car and was now trying to dry them. She waved her fingers in rapid tiny motions and periodically blew on the tips of them.

By the time I reached the door, my feet were throbbing. My mother and Vick were already inside making their way up the wide staircase to the dining room.

"Oh! My! God!" my mother turned and mouthed to me. "Can you believe it?" she whispered. "It's like *Gone with the Wind.*" She pawed at the banister with fingers spread wide, trying not to ruin her polish.

The clubhouse was old brick covered with dark-green ivy. Inside smelled like stale cigars and freshly cut grass. The ceiling was high and vaulted and when we walked on the wall-to-wall carpeting, the old hardwood floors squeaked beneath it. We sat at a table in the corner overlooking the golf course. My mother scanned the room, glowing as if she were in a deodorant commercial, exuding the confidence that she was sweet-smelling and dry. She didn't notice, but people were staring at her and nobody said hello to Vick.

Meanwhile, I was sweating. My pantyhose were making my

legs itch, and my crotch was on fire. The shoulders on the dress were so tight that I could barely reach my fork.

"Sit up," my mother whispered when I started to slouch. She caught my eye and corrected me by stiffening up herself. She raised the corners of her mouth with her forefinger and thumb, instructing me to smile. Twice, through her teeth like a ventriloquist, she inched closer to me and said, "Use your napkin." Then she covered her tracks with a grin.

The waitstaff wore red bow ties and white shirts. The men wore black pants, the women black skirts. The napkins were starched. There were too many forks and knives and spoons. "Pick one and stick with it," my mother said. "That's what I'm doing."

I tried but couldn't choke down my grass-fed burger. She was eating salmon soufflé, cozying up to Vick, repeatedly telling him how delicious it was. There was a feverishness to my mother's eagerness to please him. But I knew it would end. She and I liked McDonald's. We preferred to bring it home and eat it sitting up watching TV in bed.

Vick reached out and held my mother's hand. He looked across the table and smiled at me. "I feel so lucky," he whimpered. He'd had three martinis.

"Awww." My mother crinkled her nose at him.

God help me. I looked away.

"I mean it," he went on. "You have no idea how happy I am right now." There was a catch in his voice. I glanced across the table at him.

Vick had bad skin. To hide it, he went to a tanning booth. He had goggle-shaped pale ovals around his eyes. Now his skin was blotchy and red and his bottom lip quivered.

"It's been so long." He was wearing his napkin as a bib. He took the corner of it, lowered his head, and wiped his eyes.

Lynette had died ten years ago but, according to my mother, he missed her every day. He kept pictures of her everywhere. He still had her clothes in a spare closet in the hallway. My mother told me she'd seen him once standing in front of it, crying into the hem of a dress.

"You see," my mother whispered and tapped me on the leg, "how nice he is?" She raised her wineglass as if to say *I told you so* and took a sip.

CHAPTER THIRTY-THREE

Childhood

My Dearest Cousin Ruth,

I took a jaunt by your house and it's still empty. The front window is broken, but nothing else seemed out of place. Good news! I found your baseball cap. Shall I send it? Or keep it here for you?

P.S. I re-measured the space behind the gas station and I do think you're quite right. There is sufficient room to fit a couch up against the wall.

Yours Truly,
Lady Pam-o-lot

I missed Fat River. I missed the way our ceiling leaked and the smell of our kitchen garbage. And I missed all the sounds— the garbled words from McDonald's drive-thru, the moan of our refrigerator when it opened, the high-pitched squeak when it shut, and the squawk of our front door. Besides the thrum and sputter of the sprinkler systems, Piney Hills had just one other sound: the beep. Everything here beeped. The freezer beeped if it was open too long, the oven beeped when it was hot enough, the dishwasher beeped when it was done, and in case he couldn't tell, Vick's car beeped when he was going backward. His alarm system beeped and the numbers he pressed to get the beeping to stop beeped. An elongated beep indicated he was done. There were unidentified distant beeps—those set my teeth on edge. And at night when things weren't beeping, it was dead. No rustling critters in the woods, no *whoosh* of a distant highway, no frog or insect sounds because not even the crickets wanted to hang out here.

The nights terrified me. My room was dark and big. Where was I? And how did I get here? In the dead silence, the numbers of the digital clock on my nightstand flipped over with a loud *bang!* like gunshots. I unplugged it but the backup batteries made it buzz, and you needed a Phillips-head to get them out. I felt lost, even in the bed. It was too large and made up with duvets and duvet covers and shams and throw pillows and it was wearing a skirt—a frilly piece of purple fabric gathered at its edge. Who could sleep on such a thing?

For days I didn't. On the fourth night, I finally drifted off at five A.M. but less than an hour later, an unexpected sound bolted me upright in bed. I looked around disoriented and panicked. Then I heard it again. A low-class rattle, the kind they didn't have here, clattered in the driveway. I jumped up and looked out the window. The sun was just rising, my mother's car was being towed and my bike was still on the back of it.

I hit the ground running. I flew down the overwrought staircase and out the oversize front door. In my T-shirt and tattered pajama bottoms I sprinted down the middle of the empty street as the truck pulled away. It went over the speed bump. The bell on the handlebars came loose, ringing when it hit the ground. And the last of what I knew of home disappeared around the bend.

I braced myself on the edge of the WELCOME! sign and caught my breath. Down the street, Vick's BMW pulled out of the driveway. He went to work every day so I didn't have to see him much, but that was the only good thing about that summer. When he glided past me, he gave the horn a cheery toot-toot. When he smiled, he smiled too broadly.

I looked up to the sky and shook my open palms. *Why? Why this? Why me?*

A bird landed on the top edge of the sign. He looked around and wiggled his rump. He pointed himself in an eastward direction and as if to answer all my questions, he lifted his tail and took a dump.

My Dearest Lady Pam-o-lot, I wrote later.

> *Today he took away my sturdy old bike under the guise of being nice, claiming he'd replace it with a charmless flimsy new one. I miss you terribly but Mother will soon tire of this dreadful place, I am sure of it.*
>
> *Cheerio!*
> *Your Dearest Cousin Ruth*

> *P.S. I'm enclosing the bell. Can you see if Mel can fix it for me?*

"He's getting you a new one!" My mother chased after me as I ran back into the house. "He just ordered it yesterday." But I pushed right past her. "And he's buying me a new car!"

I sprinted up the stairs, she followed me, and I slammed my door in her face.

"Ruthie, please. I'm begging you. Come on. You're acting like a baby. We're getting brand-new ones. I mean, brand spanking new, as in: never been used. We've hardly ever had anything like that." It was true, but I didn't care. I sat up on the bed with my knees bent, scowling at her through the door.

I heard her sigh and shuffle off. A few minutes later she was back.

"Here it is," she said. A color ad for a ten-speed bike appeared under the door. "Take it." She held it by its corner and wiggled it back and forth. But I didn't bite.

"Fine," she said. Then she nudged it and sent it sliding toward me on the floor.

Before I knew it, she'd left and was back again. This time she pushed a glossy brochure for a Toyota Camry underneath the door. I heard her heels fade down the hallway. I waited and when she returned she sat down against my door. I could hear her flipping through the pages of a catalog. One by one, she circled her favorite things, tore the pages out, and before I knew it half a Crate and Barrel catalog was strewn across the hardwood floor.

I heard her get up. For a long while after, there was silence. I tiptoed over, pressed my ear against the door, but still heard nothing. So I cracked the door open. The hallway looked empty. I inched forward and stepped out.

"Gotcha!" she yelled and grabbed me. She started pinching me up and down my sides.

What was wrong with her? We'd never played this idiotic

game, not even when I was little. I pushed her away, ran down the stairs, but she followed. She chased me into the kitchen and we danced around the island until I faked her out and sprinted for the living room, where she trapped me.

"I'm going to get you!" she said, holding her hands up like claws.

Oh please! I was not a three-year-old in need of cheering up and it was a little late for her to start acting like a mother.

"When you were little," she used to say, "the sound of your laughter was like magic to me." But the truth was, when I was little she and I were almost always hungry. There wasn't much to laugh about. She never had the energy—not even for a game of peek-a-boo.

I ran past her but she caught me by my T-shirt.

"You see," she said when I finally gave in laughing, "it's not so bad here."

My stomach dropped. I shot her a look. I was not so easily swayed.

"Ruthie, come on," she called as I walked away. "I thought we were having fun."

There was nothing fun about being here. Vick *did* have a pool but it was empty. The pollen that collected on the water aggravated his allergies, so he kept it covered with a tarp. A patio of manufactured paving stones was lined with lounge chairs and umbrellas as if he was expecting a crowd, but nobody ever showed up.

Cars slid in and out through automatic garage doors and children were shuffled off. The only sign of life I'd seen so far was the woman's arm across the street. She reached it out her Lexus window at the bottom of her drive and retrieved her mail promptly every day at three.

We'd toured the house repeatedly and I'd snooped around everywhere but not a single thing was out of place. There wasn't a cup ring or scratch mark on any surface. The entire atmosphere seemed devoid of life and meaning.

My mother was fooling herself if she thought we could ever belong here. She could never keep up this act. It was too much of a stretch for her. It was stiff and boring—not anything like who she really was. But that didn't stop her from trying.

It was late afternoon the next day and we'd been watching TV for hours. Equipped with a couch that had cup holders built into the arms, Vick had a whole room designated for this activity.

"Do you see that?" my mother stood up and pointed to a commercial on TV. In it a woman bounded out of her house with piping-hot cookies on a platter. A band of bright cheering children blossomed on the scene. In an instant their pudgy hands pawed the cookies off the plate. *Yum, yum,* and they were gone.

"That's what we should be doing," my mother said as if she'd cracked some code. "I'm going to bake something and I want you to go outside and when I'm done, I'll bring it out to you."

"Don't be an idiot," I mumbled.

"You know, you can be a real jerk. You're not even trying to like it here," she fumed. "I'll have you know." She swept her hand across the scenery. "This is the American dream. And as long as we're here, we are going to try it out! Now go outside and play while I bake some goddamn cookies."

My Lady Pam-o-lot,

I cannot wait until this episode is over. It is a loathsome Disneyland here. The light has no contrast or subtlety of hue. The birds sing in engineered, vapid tones, and the sky is always flat and even. It is so pruned and fashioned it is often difficult to discern what is real and what is not. And Mother now has us playing house. She is acting the part of the parent and I the part of the child. Even if I knew how to frolic, there's no place to do it here.

Cheers,
Cousin Ruth

P.S. Can you check and see: I think I left a box of Twizzlers behind the canned tomatoes on the shelf. Make sure Mel does not steal them!

I could not believe what I did sometimes to humor my mother. I was now standing outside on Vick's lawn like an idiot. Crew-cut razor sharp in fine strands of green, signs that said KEEP OFF were posted at the edge by the street. If a single blade of crabgrass nerved its way up, he'd zip a hazmat suit on, pump a tank, and blast the monstrous patch with poison. I'd seen him do it three times already this week.

I looked around and waited for something to happen—a dog to show up or a worm to surface. But not a single thing moved.

Inside, my mother was making a clatter. I heard dishes and spoons, pots and pans banging together. I could see her through the kitchen window wiping down the granite countertops. A glint of stainless steel twinkled every time she opened the refrigerator door.

As always when my mother tried to cook, eventually something burned. Before I knew it she was darting back and forth, swatting at the smoke with her new Gucci purse. When the smoke alarm began to beep, she opened and closed the back door in quick bursts.

"What the hell are you doing out there?" she abruptly yelled when she saw me standing there.

"I'm playing! What does it look like I'm doing?"

"Well, you're not trying hard enough! Move your arms and legs a bit."

My Dearest Cousin Ruth, I heard back from Peter Pam.

I was terribly saddened to hear about your bike! What a frightful turn of events. I do hope they reused it, or, heaven forbid, recycled the parts. News from Fat River: Mel may have to close the gas station and Tiny's has now temporarily stopped serving lunch. Arlene is barely hanging on. Frank O'Malley shortchanged her on a tip which gave her a hot flash so colossal she ran him down and stabbed him in the shoulder with a fork.

P.S. Remember to breathe.

The days dragged on. I watched TV and hardly ever moved. In the evenings Vick brought home take-out—Italian, Chinese, or Mexican food, and we'd eat in his dining room, where he went on about his work. "Bear Stearns, Fannie Mae, Freddie Mac, and J.P. Morgan!" The entire financial system, he told us one night, was imploding. "But no worries here!" he said in his cornball voice, shoveling chop suey into his mouth. "Washington will bail them out!" His own company, he bragged, had emerged unscathed.

Vick took another mouthful and changed the subject. "Hey! Wasn't it a perfect day today?"

"It was!" my mother said, even though she'd spent half of it in bed.

That morning she'd gotten up and dressed, seen him off to work, then fully clothed, went back to bed. She'd claimed she wasn't feeling well. But I could tell what was really going on. Her overblown acting job was taxing her.

CHAPTER THIRTY-FOUR

Humankind

I t was one o'clock in the afternoon at the end of our second week there. My mother had just gotten out of bed. She'd taken a shower and put on fresh clothes.

"Ruthie, come here." She was peering out the kitchen window. A beat-up old car, the kind they didn't have around here, was chugging down the street. When it came to a stop in front of Vick's, the tailpipe coughed. The driver killed the engine and a blast of charcoal-colored smoke ricocheted off the pavement.

The door creaked open and through the haze, a girl emerged. Her skin was olive, her long black hair pulled back in a loose bun. She closed the door, walked around, unlocked the trunk, and took out a mop.

"Quick," my mother said, "in here," and she pulled me into the bathroom off the kitchen.

"What's wrong?" I asked.

"Shh, shh." She grabbed my shoulder and raised a finger to her mouth. "Listen," she whispered. A ring of keys clanged against the front door, then it slowly opened.

"He's got a cleaning lady," my mother whispered, widening her eyes.

"Oh my God, that's so weird."

"I know," she said.

Overnight she and I had gone from living in a one-bedroom house with major plumbing problems and a leaky roof to one that had four bedrooms and a pool. Neither one of us knew how to act here, and the presence of a cleaning lady only made it worse.

"Should we say hi to her?" I asked.

"No," my mother said. "We're supposed to act like we don't see her. We should sit on the couch, watch TV, and have her clean around us."

I smirked and shook my head as if to say, *That would never work.*

We did not belong here and the cleaning lady would know it too. We knew—because my mother used to be one—that cleaning ladies can tell all there is to know about a person by the shit they leave around.

"Okay, okay," she agreed, "so we can't do that."

"Should we help her?" I asked.

"No," my mother said. "It's not our job. We're in a totally different class now."

"Aren't we all just humans?" I asked. But she didn't answer.

"Shh! She's going upstairs," my mother reported.

We heard the vacuum cleaner thump against the risers until she reached the top. The situation had paralyzed us. We stood there frozen, listening to her every move, until my mother started getting claustrophobic.

The bathroom was tiny. The house had three of them, but

this one seemed like a toy just for show. The quaint pedestal corner sink had a set of hand towels fanned out on its edge. The soap in the dish was pristine and molded like a scallop shell. The toilet had its own cubby, the box of Kleenex on the back was snuggled in a cozy.

The bathroom had no windows and my mother was dying for a smoke but her cigarettes were upstairs so she shoved a fistful of Tic Tacs into her mouth instead. She now used them to cover up her breath because she'd lied and told Vick she didn't smoke. "What the fuck is taking her so long?" she mouthed through them.

A few minutes passed. Upstairs a cell phone rang and the cleaning lady started chatting in Spanish. "Oh, great!" My mother threw her hands up. "Who the hell is that?"

Her nicotine withdrawal was giving her the jitters. She buzzed back and forth like a fly caught between panes of glass.

The cleaning lady now started in the bathroom above us. We heard her bang around. The sink ran and the toilet flushed. She let out a low grunt and her mop fell. The wooden handle bounced twice when it hit the tile floor. She flushed the toilet again and then we heard her moaning.

"Oh my God, she's not alone," my mother said. "She's having sex up there! That's it, I've had it! Clearly we've got to learn how to treat these people." And she flung the door open.

I followed behind her as she stomped up the stairs.

The girl looked up when my mother walked in. She was kneeling on the floor with her left shoulder up against the toilet. Her hair fell across her face in oily strings. Her eyes were dark and swollen. She wore a tattered smock of faded green.

Her slip-on Keds had holes in the toes. Her name, we found out later, was Carmella.

"I sorry," she said in broken English.

When I think about my mother I see things coming loose—strands of hair and little pieces of her life falling out of her purse. But now she towered over Carmella, teeth marks from a comb in her neatly pulled-back hair. Any spunk or personality my mother had was completely obliterated by her outfit. Vick now had her wearing Lynette's clothes. The dress my mother had on was red-checked like a tablecloth and gathered in the back with a white bow. My mother and I had seen one just like it once at Target. She'd pulled it off the rack and held it up for me. "Just shoot me if you ever find me wearing this."

"I sorry," Carmella repeated. "Pregnant," and she cradled her stomach.

"Pfft," my mother sputtered with her hand on her hip. "That's no excuse," she said, and pushed past me out the door.

My mother hit a deer once. She plowed right into it on the freeway, then skidded to a stop. The deer's front leg had snapped. The broken bone punctured his skin. Just before my mother cursed and pulled away, he raised his head and looked at me, exactly as Carmella did. *Please don't leave me here like this,* his expression said.

I reached my hand out and helped Carmella up.

"Ruthie!" my mother called.

This was how my mother thought you treated people like Carmella because this was how my mother had been treated herself.

Carmella blinked. Her large brown eyes looked at me in despair. She was not that much older.

"Ruthie!" my mother called again.

I meant to introduce myself, or say, "I'm sorry," but in that moment I had no idea where I belonged or who I was.

"Ruthie!" my mother yelled again, so I went running.

CHAPTER THIRTY-FIVE

Perversion

There were more presents from Vick. He gave my mother a turquoise pendant and a watch. And then my new bike arrived.

He pulled up to the house after work with it strapped to the back of his car. When he backed up the driveway, he honked. The garage door automatically lifted and he pulled in.

My mother opened the door off the kitchen and there he was, lifting the bike off the car.

"What did I tell you?" he said, glancing over at us. "It's hot off the showroom floor."

When he got it down, he wheeled it across the garage and up the two steps right into the house.

"Isn't she amazing?" He put the kickstand down, stepped back, and admired it. "Well, what do you think?"

I stared at it, speechless.

"Ruthie." My mother tugged my arm.

I turned and looked at her. She was standing next to Vick.

His arm was around her shoulder. They beamed at me like happily married parents.

"Do you like it?" my mother asked, pointing out the bike as if I didn't see it.

I missed Fat River. I missed the pile of junk at the bottom of Peter Pam's stairs. I missed Mel and Arlene. I missed the sound of Pancake barking and I'd never forget what Dotty and Hank meant to me. I mourned everything, even the dead squirrel that fell from our ceiling, and I really missed my old bike.

But it was hard to deny how beautiful this new one was. It was sleek and shiny. The iridescent red paint glowed. The spokes gleamed in a flawless spiral pattern. Even the chain was polished. It had ten speeds and the tires were so new, they squeaked when Vick wheeled it across the kitchen floor.

"You like it?" My mother pulled on my arm again.

I looked at her, then back at Vick. His chest was puffed out and he was smiling.

"Aha!" he burst. "You like it." He pointed at me. "I can tell!" He knocked me on the shoulder as if we were pals. "You see, I'm not so bad. And I'm not done yet! Wait right here. I have something else to give you." And he hurried off.

He went out to his car and came back in with two shopping bags from Macy's.

"Here," he said, handing each one of us a bag. "You can wear them tonight at dinner."

My mother opened hers. "Oh," she swooned, "it's so sweet!" She stood and held a hideous red dress against herself.

"Oh my God," she squealed when I pulled out mine. "How cute! They match!"

"You've got to be fucking kidding me," I said to her. Who was she anyway? She went in and out of character so exhaustingly, it was hard for me to tell.

"Ruthie!" she scolded with an authoritative tone she seemed to have just acquired. "Watch your language." There was no swearing around Vick. My mother simply would not have it. She'd expunged the word *fuck* from her vocabulary. Without it, an essential part of her—an arm or a leg—seemed missing.

She glared at me, then smiled at him as if to say she was sorry for my behavior.

I let out a groan and bolted upstairs for my room.

"Come on, Ruthie." My mother ran after me. "So he doesn't have the best taste in clothes." She reached out and caught me by the wrist. I spun around, pulled away, crossed my arms, and looked up at the ceiling.

"You know, the guy just bought you a brand-new bike. Focus on that! For Chrissake, why can't you just accept that life is full of compromises? And wearing shit you don't want to might just be one of them."

She was changing already, ripping her old clothes off and getting into her new ones. "Look," she continued, zipping herself up the side. "Is Gucci my favorite? No. And a year ago, do you think I'd have been caught dead wearing this? No. But I'm trying to make the best of it here. And you're not helping."

The dress made it hard for me to listen to her. It was a disturbing combination of something a five-year-old and a whore might wear. Except for the severely plunging neckline, it was totally girlish. It had tiny white bows sewn all over it, a billowy pleated skirt, and prissy puff sleeves. It looked ridiculous on her.

"Ruthie," my mother said, "look at me." She grabbed my chin. "Don't you see? Things are different now. People are dying out there."

I looked at her, her eyes ablaze. And I knew in that moment she was right. We had watched CNN. Whole segments of the population were going under. And, we knew all too well, no one would save them when they drowned.

I had heard more news from Peter Pam.

My Dearest Cousin Ruth,

Miss Frankfurt has been forced into early retirement due to budget cuts and Arlene has moved to Pennsylvania. Her rent went up and she couldn't afford it. She now lives with her sister who she hates.

Lovingly,
Lady Pam-o-lot

My chin quivered.

"Don't do it, Ruthie. I mean it. A stiff upper lip is what you need now." We were like Jews pretending to be German Catholics.

"Here," my mother said, handing me my dress. "And it wouldn't hurt you to smile. Now pucker up." She suddenly produced her lipstick. A loud *pop*, the top came off, and the tube headed for me in midair. "A little color will do you good."

That night my mother served her first pot roast and made a big to-do over it. Vick had ordered a DVD and set up a laptop on the kitchen counter and she'd been taking cooking lessons. Lynette apparently made an excellent roast, so he had my mother start with that.

She arranged the meat on the platter just so and instructed me to follow her with a towel draped across my arm as if I were her busboy.

"Are you ready?" my mother called from the kitchen.

"Ready!" Vick called back.

Dear Lady Pam-o-lot,
 It is never ending here.

 Ta-ta,
 Your beloved Cousin Ruth.

 P.S. Can you send me more Britishisms? I am running out of them.

"See?" my mother smiled, looking over her shoulder as I trudged behind her. "I could be a chef if I wanted to." She was trying to make me laugh, but my sense of humor had vanished.

Sorrow flooded me. As I watched the roast slide around on the platter, I thought about the cow and how she must have shuddered just before they slaughtered her.

"Close your eyes!" my mother yelled to Vick.

A dirge played inside my head as I paced around the table and took my seat. "Here it is!" She set the pot roast down in front of him.

"Beautiful!" he thundered and my mother's cheeks bloomed. Then he stabbed the meat and cut it into pieces. He *mmmmed* and chewed and raised his eyebrows at my mother in overdone expressions of enjoyment throughout the meal.

I had to admit, it wasn't every day my mother cooked something that didn't look as if it had been involved in a minor explosion, and I tried, but I just couldn't swallow it.

"You know," Vick said in between his chewing, "my aunt Agnes used to make an excellent roast." I rolled my eyes. Here we go again. We had been there less than three weeks and I'd heard way too much about his aunt Agnes already. "Agnes was a saint!" he'd boom in his two-martini voice.

Vick had grown up in Oklahoma. His mother died in childbirth and his father disappeared after that. It made my mother snivel. "He's suffered so much tragedy."

He was raised by Agnes and he'd go on not only about Agnes but about her ancestors too. They came over on the Mayflower; they worked in the mills in Lowell, Massachusetts. They moved west looking for land.

Agnes had been the oldest of ten. When Agnes's mother died, Agnes raised her younger siblings and when she was done with them, she raised him. She never married, she never complained, and she kept canaries, which was why half the shit Vick owned—his bathrobe, his dish towels, his plates and cloth napkins—had little yellow birds on them.

He always delivered his Agnes stories like sermons, but he told this one with extra zeal. He got carried away in her tale of martyrdom and when he told us how she died—"alone in a fire!"—he shuddered. "Can you believe that? Why not peacefully in her sleep?" Horrified, his face twisted up. All of his Agnes stories upset him, but this time he lowered his head and wept.

My mother got up, put her arm around him, and rocked him gently in his seat. Mostly he was just pathetic to me, but that night I felt sorry for him.

"Get him some water," my mother said, so I did.

When I returned he drank it in one gulp. "Thank you." He looked up at me. "Both of you." He snuggled into the crook of my mother's arms. "You mean so much to me."

Vick was boisterous and overly affable. But he didn't seem to have friends. When he golfed, he didn't have a regular group. He'd sign up at the pro shop and only got called if someone needed a player. When he drove through Piney Hills, he honked and waved at all his neighbors. Sometimes he rolled his window down and shouted corny things like "Beautiful day!" or "Life is looking up!" But nobody invited him to dinner.

One day I looked out and saw him gassing a weed. An orange inflatable ball rolled by him on his lawn. Vick looked across the street. A kid had gotten loose and when Vick saw him standing on his driveway looking longingly at his ball, Vick's eyes lit up. He smiled his widest grin. In his hazmat suit, with his queer walk-run, he cut across the grass and picked the ball up. He was just about to roll it back to the boy when the boy's mother swooped down. She gave Vick a look like she wanted nothing to do with him. She gathered her son, whisked him off, and sealed him back inside again.

That night at the dinner table with my mother by his side, he took my wrist and pulled me closer. With the two of us huddled into him he sniveled. "You are my family now." He moved his hand up the zipper on my dress and a shiver ran up my spine. The chill went right through me.

CHAPTER THIRTY-SIX

Preservation

. . . twenty-eight, twenty-nine, thirty." I huffed. I was doing push-ups in my room.

Dear Lady Pam-o-lot, I composed inside my head.

The charade is finally waning. Mother still plasters on a smile when he boasts about his golf game, but a grave expression sometimes grips her face when he smiles at me. I can no longer wait, though. I may have to drug her to get her out and I will kill him if I have to.

Your Dearly Beloved Cousin Ruth

P.S. Do you believe in miracles? It occurred to me that I never asked you and I really want to know.

I had to get us out of here. I wasn't sure how, but I was preparing myself. I developed a high-intensity aerobics routine and I did the routine twice a day. If I worked myself up into a big enough sweat, my fear would dissolve into a sense of calm and power.

I put myself on a fat-free, sugar-free, cholesterol-free diet and I started building up my lung capacity by holding my breath until I almost fainted. And even when I wasn't doing anything, like when I watched TV, I'd squeeze my stomach muscles tight and hold them. Basically, I was always improving and I was training my brain. When Vick looked at me, I looked right back at him. I'd pick a spot on his forehead and imagine seeing smoke as my eyes bored a hole through his skull.

I flipped over and started doing crunches. I was blasting through them when my mother stumbled through the door.

With her new Gucci bag slung over her shoulder, she careened across the room, aiming a goblet of wine for the night table. Half of it sloshed out and hit the wall as she set it down. It was only four o'clock.

She sat on the edge of the bed teetering. Her hair had almost completely fallen out of her bun. She reached back, gathered it off her neck, and futilely tucked it in. Then she fumbled through her bag, pulled out a cigarette, an ashtray, and an aerosol can of Glade. She struck a match but her hands shook and the match went out. She went through five matches, tossing and missing the ashtray with each one. When she finally got one lit, she widened the V of her fingers, pinched the cigarette between her lips, and inhaled hard. Her cheeks caved in and her shoulders dropped as if she'd just breathed in the sweet smell of roses. When she blew the smoke out, she picked up the aerosol can and gassed it away with a mist of lemon Glade. He still didn't think she smoked, but she'd gotten tired of standing outside, so this was how she did it now. The vapors made me choke, but the nicotine pepped her up a bit.

"So I'm through with yoga," she said. She'd taken it up for only a day. Early one morning she watched a supermodel do it. But my mother couldn't even hold child's pose, so she immediately quit. "And I'm not going to do crocheting either. I'm taking up felting instead," she slurred. "Vick showed me a hat Lynette made. You should see how cute it is."

I didn't bother to comment. I had moved on to my isometric squats and lunges. With my hands on my hips, I made my way across the room. With each stride, I stepped a little lower so I could feel my legs burn.

A thin smile traced my mother's lips as she changed the subject. "When I see you in your cap and gown walk across the stage, I'll be whooping and hollering." She raised a finger and twirled it around like a noisemaker. "'That's my daughter!' I'm gonna shout." She blasted away another cloud of smoke, then took a swig of wine. "Yup," she said, "that's how I'll know that this life of mine was worth something."

I broke out into jumping jacks and grunted through them. Jumping jacks were not part of my normal routine, but I'd eaten a cookie that day so I was really pushing it.

My mother finished her cigarette and stuffed a handful of Tic Tacs into her mouth. "I'm so proud of you," she mumbled, tilting her head to keep the mints from tumbling out. She slugged back some wine and unconsciously swallowed them like pills.

She lit another cigarette and exhaled. Her mouth twisted. Then she started in. "If anything ever happened to you, I would *die*," she said with an emphatic spritz of the air freshener. But she was drunker now and her aim was off so the cloud of smoke floated to the ceiling while the mist of Glade hit the ground.

"And if anyone ever lays a hand on you, I'll kill them!" She guzzled the rest of her wine and banged the glass down.

I made quick little pumping motions with my arms and concentrated on my breathing. My face was red-hot. My temples throbbed. I could feel oxygen coursing through my arteries.

"You know that, don't you?" she asked. "Don't you?"

I kept jumping. *Faster, faster, faster.* I could not believe how fast I was going. Adrenaline flooded me. I felt as if I could fly. Not a single thing could weigh me down.

"DON'T YOU?" she screamed at the top of her lungs.

A smoky, alcoholic fume mushroomed from her mouth. As she raised her can of Glade, the tiny spray nozzle closed in on me and a haze of lemon gassed me. At first I felt my limbs propel me up, then—*bam!*—like that, I hit the ground.

Five minutes or an hour could have passed, I couldn't tell. But when my eyes slowly opened, my mother was there. She seemed sober now, kneeling next to me, dabbing my forehead with a washcloth like a nurse.

"You're okay," she said. She'd tucked a pillow under my head. "Here." She reached up and grabbed a cup of ginger ale off the night table. "Have some." She cradled my head in her hand, raised me up, and held a straw to my lips, then gently laid me down again.

The sprinklers went on outside and the sound of shooting water pulsed up and down the street. The fading daylight moved across the room in tints of orange.

My mother cupped her hand around my face, then bent over and kissed me on the forehead.

"Your nose is cold." She pulled a blanket off the bed. "Come here, I'll warm you up." She wrapped herself around me.

The sound of the sprinkler system outside slowed. The synchronized arcs of water fell. The sun lowered in the sky and swaddled us in bluish gold.

Piney Hills was a deadening place. But that afternoon, something shifted. I could tell by the way my mother looked off into the distance, her wheels were turning. She and I would leave this place and laugh at it someday. The only question now was when.

CHAPTER THIRTY-SEVEN

Purgatory

N o matter how hard I tried not to, I could always hear them having sex. With formulaic rhythm, my mother's manufactured high-pitched whimper would slowly bloom into a vapid, overdone crescendo.

Then I'd wait. With every guy we'd ever lived with, I'd eventually hear the sound of her feet, *pat, pat, pat*, as she made her way across the hallway. "Push over," she'd say to me. "I can't sleep." And this was how I knew for sure the end was near. She and I would eventually leave together and the warrior that was my mother would reappear.

The moonlight sank below the houses and the long angled shadows traveled westward up the street. It was a Friday night when I finally heard the shuffle of bare feet coming toward me on the carpet. We'd been at Vick's for almost a month by then.

My bedroom door slowly opened.

"Mom?" I said.

In my mind, I will forever see the two of us sitting up in bed. I can picture her gathering her hair and laying it back down on the pillow behind her. I hear us laughing as she recounts all the crazy things we'd done together. And I can see the tip of her cigarette—how it lit up her face when she smoked, how it waved around and rested between her two fingers as if it had always been there, a graceful part of her hand. And I would think: there was nothing I ever wanted more than to sit and watch my mother smoke.

"Mom?" I asked again.

A figure stood by me.

"Push over," I waited to hear.

But in the dark I realized it was Vick standing over me. The waning moonlight inside the room gave his face a purple glow.

My heart began to pound. There was a drumming in my ears. My throat closed up. Bits and pieces of my life flashed in my mind: the California skyline, the gap in my mother's smile where she was missing her tooth, Peter Pam's mules, Patti's ponytail.

I was afraid to move. My eyes drifted down expecting to see an axe in his hand, but instead I came face-to-face with something far worse.

Vick's erection bounced in the pup tent of his pajamas. The little yellow birds printed on the fabric winked as they rode up and down.

I looked at his face again. He was shaking now. He winced and sucked his bottom lip in. His eyes were moist and pleading as if to say, *I am mortified by what I want to do.*

✧

Enh!—Enh!—Enh! My adrenaline kicked in and an alarm went off inside my head. *Procure the fireplace poker just in case,* Peter

Pam had written in her last letter. And I had. I jumped up away from him, dropped to the floor, and reached under the bed where I kept it. I grabbed the handle, stood up, and wielded it above my head. I was going to kill him if I had to. I lifted the poker higher, but then something stopped me.

My mother, I realized, was standing in the doorway. A stripe of moonlight trailed along the wall and fell across her face.

Vick turned and saw her. His cheeks glowed bright red. "I was just leaving," he said. Hunched over and covering his erection, he scurried out the door like a rat.

I dropped the poker. My mother barely looked at me before she turned and followed him. There was no time to plot things out. She and I both knew the drill.

"This is my daughter, Ruth." With every guy we'd ever lived with, this was how she'd introduce me, simply as Ruth. "Now, I don't know where you and me are going"—she'd point back and forth between him and her and curl her lip—"but you ever try laying a hand on her and I will kill you." That night in Fat River hadn't been the first time my mother threatened a guy with a gun.

With the same garbage bags I used when we moved from Fat River, I ran around feverishly packing. I stuffed my clothes into the bags and, on the dresser where I kept them, I gathered up my Mary figurines. In the middle of the night, she would come and get me.

I imagined we'd tie Vick up, steal his car, and douse his house with gasoline. I could hear our tires squeal, spinning backwards down the driveway, where my mother would pause long enough for me to strike and throw the match. She'd shift the car, and as we lurched forward, she'd flip her middle finger out the window and yell "Fuck you!" to the insolent squirrels flanking his driveway. Then the house would explode. Silhouetted by the yellow moon we'd streak across the earth and the sound of our triumphant laughter would fill the streets.

With an overstuffed garbage bag under each arm and the poker lying across my knees, I sat up and waited. In increments, the night sky lightened. The afterglow of my mother lingered in the doorway until the sun rose, but she never came to get me.

CHAPTER THIRTY-EIGHT

Denial

In the morning, he was gone and my mother was sitting at the kitchen table drinking coffee. Her back was to me. Her legs were crossed. A swirl of steam rose off her mug. A bottle of rum sat at her elbow. She was waving her hands as if she were speaking to someone across from her, telling them something urgent.

It was still early, but she was already in a dress, floral print and not her style, but it's what my mother did now: she got up, like Lynette, every morning and put on something nice.

She paused, lifted a hand, and hooked her hair behind her ear. It was a familiar gesture, but I wasn't sure anymore who was doing it.

"Mom?" I said, but she didn't hear me. She cocked her head. She shrugged and held her palms up: *beats me.*

"Mom?" I repeated. My chin began to quiver. "Can we please go now?"

She and I used to find things in other people's garbage. When I was six, we found a whole bag filled with clothes that fit us perfectly. We wore them for two days until we discovered they were infested with bugs. She had to steal lice shampoo from Walgreens and wash us in a Burger King bathroom. Then there was the time when a cop caught her urinating in an alley and wouldn't let her go until she showed him her "titties." And there were all the nights we couldn't sleep because our hunger pains kept us up.

A lifetime of humiliating poverty had left a laceration on her soul. And it was all there, written on her face, when she turned around and looked at me.

She was gaunt. Her eyes were swollen. Bits of her broken life were scattered inside them in shards like shattered glass.

Please, Mom, I started to say. But she looked away.

"I was just about to make some pancakes," my mother said, getting up and hustling by me. "I know exactly how to do it now." She prattled on, opening drawers, pawing through utensils. "So they're nice and fluffy, not too dry, not too moist. I'll make them golden brown. I saw it on this cooking show. It's all in the wrist when you whisk the batter. And you can't just use a fork." She pulled out a whisk and raised it up. "Using a fork is like using a pencil when a thick Magic Marker is really what you need."

She buzzed around the kitchen, opening and closing the cupboards and pulling things out. A maze of words spilled from her mouth and landed at my feet. It was impossible to make sense of what she said. She bounced around from Magic Markers to paper towels to skydiving and then to Paris Hilton. I listened closely for transitions, but there were none.

CHAPTER THIRTY-NINE

Sacrifice

Q uick," my mother said, "get your bags." It was two days later in the middle of the night and she was pulling me out of bed.

Dear Sir Pam-o-lot, we are coming home at last!

P.S. What's your opinion? Shall we paint the room in the back of the gas station blue or red?

I should never have doubted her. She might stray or crash and burn or need a place to rest, but in the end my mother always rises.

"I gave him extra sleeping pills. We gotta make it fast before they wear off."

I dragged my garbage bags and followed her. With a flashlight in her hand, we snuck through the house like thieves. I lagged behind, looking around for something to steal.

"There's no time for that," my mother said when she saw me. "Here, stick this in your pocket." She gave me a wad of cash. "I swiped it off his dresser."

At the door to the garage she handed me the flashlight. Holding up a piece of paper, she punched the combination into the keypad and the door swung open. She'd stolen his car keys. We slid into the seats, and with the press of a button, the garage door lifted and she and I were out.

We sped through the night. This time, the ride was much nicer. Nothing banged or rattled in a BMW. The tires slithered soundlessly on the surface of the road like a snake across a pond.

As if a ream of fabric had been stretched across it, the sky was black and solid. When we were far enough away, light seeped through and the pulse of life returned. The soothing sound of cars rushed on a distant highway. The sky became full of complicated grays and dappled warm tones of bare earth replaced the blinding green.

At long last, we were on the road again together. That was all that mattered. I sighed, relieved. My shoulders dropped. The silhouette of my mother's profile in the driver's seat eased me into a dreamy, peaceful sleep.

"Wake up, Ruthie. Come on." My mother reached across me, opened my door, then ran around to pull me out.

I was still half asleep as she led me through a parking lot. I remember the smell of gasoline and the flickering of streetlights overhead.

My mother pushed open a door and pulled me through. A blast of light blinded me. Our footsteps echoed on the concrete floor. When she finally stopped, I rubbed my eyes and looked around. The ceiling was vaulted with metal beams. Overhead a fan wheezed. A passerby hit my shoulder. An old lady shuffled behind him. Her chin hairs caught the light. A dreary couple sat on a wooden bench against the wall, a worn-out duffle bag between them. A big woman with a double chin big enough to fit a second face pulled a tiny suitcase with a missing wheel. When it left my line of vision, a large pair of women's shoes was there. A cardboard box with handles sat beside them on the floor.

The owner bent to pick the box up and a meow inside soared soprano. Pigeons scattered in the rafters.

My eyes traveled up the woman's arm and standing right in front of me was Peter Pam. I looked around, confused, then startled when I realized where I was. We were in a bus station. I turned to find my mother, but she had vanished. A pigeon feather drifted down and landed in the place where I last saw her.

Epilogue

The September sunlight dapples and moves in mesmerizing patterns. A dusting of yellow light catches the tops of the trees as if an angel had grazed them with spray paint. A breeze cuts across the campus and cools my cheeks. It is five years later and I am standing in Cambridge, Massachusetts, on the edge of Harvard Yard.

Peter Pam was holding two tickets for Boston that day. My mother had charged them on Vick's credit card and sent them to her with a note to meet us. Tiny's, Peter Pam had told me, was closing, so she was ready to leave Fat River anyway.

We live together in a basement apartment in Somerville where Peter Pam's waitressing career really took off. The place she works has horrible food, but throngs of people go there just to see her. Recently Peter Pam's boyfriend, Doug, moved in with us. Doug and I get along famously and he is so sweet with Peter Pam. I hope someday to meet someone myself, but I don't trust women and I'm afraid of men. I have a dog, though. I found her on the street, a scrawny frightened little girl we named Tara.

We loved her up and fed her, and that was all it took. She's now plump and happy and Dave the cat is in love with her. They sleep snuggled up together on the couch. The five of us make a family and that's all I really need.

For a long time, without my mother half of me felt missing, the half that knew how to relate and laugh and joke. My mother, I knew, did what she thought she had to, but the pain of it nearly killed us both.

When she called, she'd fill the space between us with idle chit-chat or she'd repeat an episode of a TV show verbatim. Sometimes she'd recount a crazy thing we'd done together. She hid behind her laughter, but I could hear the sorrow in her voice. "I miss you," she always said to me.

For a while she sent me letters twice a week. And she'd tuck all kinds of things into them: a picture she'd clipped from a magazine with a sticky note, "Isn't this funny?" Or an article about a celebrity from *People* magazine. And always there were coupons. Land O'Lakes butter and Philips light bulbs, Maxwell House coffee and Brawny paper towels—anything she thought I might need. Once a month, she'd send me cash. Vick kept his billfold on his dresser, she'd explained to me, and my mother stole a little every week.

She came to see me twice; each time she looked a little thinner. More and more when I spoke to her, she was drunk. She'd slur her words, telling me how much she really loved Vick, then ranting on about how she hated him.

Her fatigue grew progressively worse. Her cough became more violent, and two years ago when they discovered a tumor in her lung, she had no strength left to fight it. She swallowed a fistful of sleeping pills and washed them down with bourbon. Vick found her face up in the middle of the tarp covering his empty pool as if she'd died searching for a place to get cool.

I buried her in Fat River. I made sure she was wearing heels and so she went with plenty of color, I took handfuls of the most brilliant confetti and sprinkled it in her casket.

Mel and Svetlana flew back for the funeral from Florida, where they now live. Arlene drove up from Pennsylvania. Miss Frankfurt came too. It made my heart ache to have us all together. Vick, of course, wailed. People emptied their pockets of Kleenex for him but he carried on, blowing his nose like an old lady.

A box from my mother arrived for me a few days after she died. Inside was her old pocketbook, two pairs of earrings, a wristwatch she'd told me once belonged to her mother, the Virgin Mary that had been glued to our dashboard, and a Polaroid of the moment right after I was born. In it, my mother was reaching forward. A pair of hands held me up to her. Like a ribbon of visible music, the umbilical cord still joined us. Stuck to the bottom was a Post-It note with her last words to me scribbled on it. "I'm so proud of you," it said.

It took me years to finish high school. I lost interest in writing papers. I kept dropping out and reenrolling. For a long time, not even Peter Pam could cheer me up. But here I finally am.

The trees that line the Harvard walkways are full and healthy. Their tender leaves grow on low branches in clumps like clouds. A tower clock chimes. A group of students walks right by me. Someone's shoulder knocks mine. I turn around, but no one stops.

✧

The meek shall inherit the earth, the Bible says, but how many have to suffer first? Where I come from, children are wrenched away from homes. Men are disposable, boys are lost, women are beaten or killed. Little girls are left quaking at the sight of so much blood. And we blame them when they become less than perfect mothers. The meek shall inherit the earth, but why can't we just share it?

This was the beginning of the essay I wrote that got me my interview at Harvard. My appointment is at three and I came here straight from work. Religion is what I want to study, and I already know what I'd do for my senior thesis project. I'd deconstruct the Bible and point out all its flaws.

A sparrow hovers overhead. It plummets to the ground a few feet in front of me. I look up to see where it came from and find myself thinking about my mother. Always, I feel her watching me. I remember a night in Fat River. It was after midnight and she and I were in our lounge chairs looking up at the sky. "We're so lucky," my mother had said. It was hard for us to believe that life could be so good.

I look down at the bird again. I am sure it's dead. But its eye opens. It blinks and looks around. The beak lets out a timid chirp. The bird gets up, hops about, and, as if not a single thing had happened, it lifts off the ground. I raise my head and follow it. The silvery undersides of its wings flicker in the sunlight, until it finds its flock and they soar off together like a thousand hopeful minnows in the sea.

Acknowledgments

Many thanks to all those who provided support, read my book, and offered feedback. Thank you to my good friends Jack Coyle, Carol Previte, and Jim Chiros for reassuring me the book was done. Thanks to Becca Kauffman and especially Alex Leake, who calmed me down and helped me cross the finish line. My gratitude to Helen Brann and the late Joan Parker for their friendship, advice, and wisdom. Thanks to Lou Goodman for his amazing work and Janice and Debra Barsha for their enthusiasm and support. I am grateful to the people who have guided me, especially my fifth-grade teacher William Schoen and Robert Alter. And to my brother, Andrew, who has taught me how to live with grace and humor. I am indebted to my team at Scribner: Whitney Frick, Paul Whitlatch, Lauren Hughes, Katie Monaghan, Tal Goretsky. My deepest gratitude to my agent, Esther Newberg, whose interest in my work has changed everything. And to Joyce Kauffman: I am eternally grateful for all that you are and all that you have given me.

All We Had

A Novel

ANNIE WEATHERWAX

Introduction

Teetering on the brink of homelessness at the height of the housing boom, thirteen-year-old Ruthie Carmichael and her mother, Rita, load up their possessions (and a few stolen goods) in their battered Ford Escort and set out cross-country in search of a better life. When car trouble brings their journey to an end in the small town of Fat River, they unexpectedly find a home amid the town's quirky residents. At its core, *All We Had* is a love story between a mother and daughter whose bond is irrevocably altered by their search for the elusive American Dream.

Topics and Questions for Discussion

1. Describe Ruthie and Rita's relationship. How is it traditional and how is it unusual? Rita's shortcomings as a parent are often evident, but in what ways is she a good mother? What kind of mothering do you think she had?

2. What is "fierce and smart" about Rita? Why does Rita hide these traits from men in particular? How do economic circumstances inform this behavior?

3. Rita and Ruthie's car is central to their lives. For a long time it's the only thing they own, and when they have no other choice, it doubles as their home. In what other ways is the car significant?

4. Ruthie's heroes are Hillary Clinton, Anne Frank, and the Virgin Mary. Why do you suppose she's drawn to these female figures? What does each one of them represent to her?

5. How does the economic stability Rita and Ruthie find in Fat River change them? How does it impact their view of themselves, their relationship with each other, and their view of the people around them?

6. How do the people Rita and Ruthie meet in Fat River, including Mel, Patti, Arlene, Peter Pam, and the Hansons, influence them?

7. What role does Mel play in Ruthie's life? In what way does he change Ruthie's view of men?

8. Peter Pam is described as the novel's voice of warmth and reason. Why do you think this is, and in what ways is this unexpected? Why do you think Ruthie develops such a close friendship with her?

9. When Peter Pam is attacked outside the diner, why does Ruthie take matters into her own hands rather than seek help? What does this reveal about Ruthie and the ways in which her upbringing has shaped her?

10. In this same scene, Rita appears more than willing to come to her daughter's defense. How and why does this change at the end of the novel?

11. Discuss Miss Frankfurt's small yet important role in the story. Why does she go out of her way to help Ruthie and Rita, as well as convince Peter to resume being Peter Pam?

12. The book takes place in a small American town set in the shadow of Walmart. Discuss the role Walmart plays in the book. What is the significance of the scene in Walmart?

13. *All We Had* is set during the recent subprime mortgage crisis, which affected families across the country and made headline news. How does the economic decline of Fat River change its residents? How does it impact their relationships?

14. How and why does Ruthie and Rita's relationship change once Vick enters the picture?

15. Vick has a pool, but the pool is empty, and Piney Hills, where he lives, has neither pine trees nor hills. In what other ways is the reality of Rita and Ruthie's lives distorted here?

16. What motivates Rita to send Ruthie away? Was it selfish or selfless of her to let Ruthie go?

17. In what ways does Ruthie's voice impact this novel? How do her insights, humor, and observations color and shape this story?

18. Homeownership was once thought to be a pathway out of poverty. Do you think it still is? What is the novel's overall message about economic inequality? Has reading *All We Had* changed your view of poverty?